JOE
THE HOTEL BOY

OR

WINNING OUT BY PLUCK

HORATIO ALGER, JR.

Joe The Hotel Boy

Horatio Alger Jr.

© 1st World Library – Literary Society, 2004
PO Box 2211
Fairfield, IA 52556
www.1stworldlibrary.org
First Edition

LCCN: 2004195313

Softcover ISBN: 1-4218-0144-2
Hardcover ISBN: 1-4218-0044-6
eBook ISBN: 1-4218-0244-9

Purchase *"Joe The Hotel Boy"*
as a traditional bound book at:
www.1stWorldLibrary.org/purchase.asp?ISBN=1-4218-0144-2

1st World Library Literary Society is a nonprofit
organization dedicated to promoting literacy by:

- Creating a free internet library accessible from any
  computer worldwide.
- Hosting writing competitions and offering book
  publishing scholarships.

Joe The Hotel Boy
contributed by Tim, Ed & Rodney
in support of
1st World Library Literary Society

CONTENTS.

PREFACE.

A number of years ago the author of this story set out to depict life among the boys of a great city, and especially among those who had to make their own way in the world. Among those already described are the ways of newsboys, match boys, peddlers, street musicians, and many others.

In the present tale are related the adventures of a country lad who, after living for some time with a strange hermit, goes forth into the world and finds work, first in a summer hotel and then in a large hotel in the city. Joe finds his road no easy one to travel, and he has to face not a few hardships, but in the end all turns out well.

It may be added here that many of the happenings told of in this story, odd as they may seem, are taken from life. Truth is indeed stranger than fiction, and life itself is full of romance from start to finish.

If there is a moral to be drawn from this story, it is a twofold one, namely, that honesty is always the best policy, and that if one wishes to succeed in life he must stick at his work steadily and watch every opportunity for advancement.

CHAPTER I.

OUT IN A STORM.

"What do you think of this storm, Joe?"

"I think it is going to be a heavy one, Ned. I wish we were back home," replied Joe Bodley, as he looked at the heavy clouds which overhung Lake Tandy.

"Do you think we'll catch much rain before we get back?" And Ned, who was the son of a rich man and well dressed, looked at the new suit of clothes that he wore.

"I'm afraid we shall, Ned. Those black clouds back of Mount Sam mean something." "If this new suit gets soaked it will be ruined," grumbled Ned, and gave a sigh.

"I am sorry for the suit, Ned; but I didn't think it was going to rain when we started."

"Oh, I am not blaming you, Joe. It looked clear enough this morning. Can't we get to some sort of shelter before the rain reaches us?"

"We can try."

"Which is the nearest shelter?"

Joe Bodley mused for a moment.

"The nearest that I know of is over at yonder point, Ned. It's an old hunting lodge that used to belong to the Cameron family. It has been deserted for several years."

"Then let us row for that place, and be quick about it," said Ned Talmadge. "I am not going to get wet if I can help it."

As he spoke he took up a pair of oars lying in the big rowboat he and Joe Bodley occupied. Joe was already rowing and the rich boy joined in, and the craft was headed for the spot Joe had pointed out.

The lake was one located in the central part of the State of Pennsylvania. It was perhaps a mile wide and more than that long, and surrounded by mountains and long ranges of hills. At the lower end of the lake was a small settlement of scant importance and at the upper end, where there was a stream of no mean size, was the town of Riverside. At Riverside were situated several summer hotels and boarding houses, and also the elegant mansion in which Ned Talmadge resided, with his parents and his four sisters.

Joe Bodley was as poor as Ned Talmadge was rich, yet the two lads were quite friendly. Joe knew a good deal about hunting and fishing, and also knew all about handling boats. They frequently went out together, and Ned insisted upon paying the poorer boy for all extra services.

Joe's home was located on the side of the mountain which was just now wrapped in such dark and ominous looking clouds. He lived with Hiram Bodley, an old man who was a hermit. The home consisted of a cabin of two rooms, scantily furnished. Hiram Bodley had been a hunter and guide, but of late years rheumatism had kept him from doing work and Joe was largely the support of the pair, - taking out pleasure parties for pay whenever he could, and fishing and hunting in the between times, and using or selling what was gained thereby.

There was a good deal of a mystery surrounding Joe's parentage. It was claimed that he was a nephew of Hiram Bodley, and that, after the death of his mother and sisters, his father had drifted out to California and then to Australia. What the real truth concerning him was we shall learn later.

Joe was a boy of twelve, but constant life in the open air had made him tall and strong and he looked to be several years older.

He had dark eyes and hair, and was much tanned by the sun. The rowboat had been out a good distance on the lake and a minute before the shore was gained the large drops of rain began to fall.

"We are going to get wet after all!" cried Ned, chagrined.

"Pull for all you are worth and we'll soon be under the trees," answered Joe.

They bent to the oars, and a dozen more strokes sent the rowboat under a clump of pines growing close to the edge of the lake. Just as the boat struck the bank and Ned leaped out there came a great downpour which made the surface of Lake Tandy fairly sizzle.

"Run to the lodge, Ned; I'll look after the boat!" shouted Joe.

"But you'll get wet."

"Never mind; run, I tell you!"

Thus admonished, Ned ran for the old hunting lodge, which was situated about two hundred feet away. Joe remained behind long enough to secure the rowboat and the oars and then he followed his friend.

Just as one porch of the old lodge was reached there came a flash of lightning, followed by a clap of thunder that made Ned jump. Then followed more thunder and lightning, and the rain came down steadily.

"Ugh! I must say I don't like this at all," remarked Ned, as he crouched in a corner of the shelter. "I hope the lightning doesn't strike this place."

"We can be thankful that we were not caught out in the middle of the lake, Ned."

"I agree on that, Joe, - but it doesn't help matters much. Oh, dear me!" And Ned shrank down, as another blinding flash of lightning lit up the scene.

It was not a comfortable situation and Joe did not like it any more than did his friend. But the hermit's boy was accustomed to being out in the elements, and therefore was not so impressed by what was taking place.

"The rain will fill the boat," said Ned, presently.

"Never mind, we can easily bail her out or turn her over."

"When do you think this storm will stop?"

"In an hour or two, most likely. Such storms never last very long. What time is it, Ned?"

"Half-past two," answered Ned, after consulting the handsome watch he carried.

"Then, if it clears in two hours, we'll have plenty of time to get home before dark."

"I don't care to stay here two hours," grumbled Ned. "It's not a very inviting place."

"It's better than being out under the trees," answered Joe, cheerfully. The hermit's boy was always ready to look on the brighter side of things.

"Oh, of course."

"And we have a fine string of fish, don't forget that, Ned. We were lucky to get so many before the storm came up."

"Do you want the fish, or are you going to let me take them?"

"I'd like to have one fish. You may take the others."

"Not unless you let me pay for them, Joe."

"Oh, you needn't mind about paying me."

"But I insist," came from Ned. "I won't touch them otherwise."

"All right, you can pay me for what I caught."

"No, I want to pay for all of them. Your time is worth something, and I know you have to support your - the old hermit now."

"All right, Ned, have your own way. Yes, I admit, I need all the money I get."

"Is the old hermit very sick?"

"Not so sick, but his rheumatism keeps him from going out hunting or fishing, so all that work falls to me."

"It's a good deal on your shoulders, Joe."

"I make the best of it, for there is nothing else to do."

"By the way, Joe, you once spoke to me about - well, about yourself," went on Ned, after some hesitation. "Did you ever learn anything more? You need not tell me if you don't care to."

At these words Joe's face clouded for an instant.

"No, I haven't learned a thing more, Ned."

"Then you don't really know if you are the hermit's nephew or not?"

"Oh, I think I am, but I don't know whatever became of my father."

"Does the hermit think he is alive?"

"He doesn't know, and he hasn't any means of finding out."

"Well, if I were you, I'd find out, some way or other."

"I'm going to find out - some day," replied Joe. "But, to tell the truth, I don't know how to go at it. Uncle Hiram doesn't like to talk about it. He thinks my father did wrong to go away.

I imagine they had a quarrel over it."

"Has he ever heard from your father since?"

"Not a word."

"Did he write?"

"He didn't know where to write to."

"Humph! It is certainly a mystery, Joe."

"You are right, Ned; and as I said before, I am going to solve it some time, even if it takes years of work to do it," replied the hermit's boy.

CHAPTER II.

A MYSTERIOUS CONVERSATION.

The old hunting lodge where the two boys had sought shelter was a rambling affair, consisting of a square building built of logs, and half a dozen wings, running to the rear and to one side. There were also two piazzas, and a shed, where wood had been kept for winter use.

"In another year or two this old lodge will fall down," remarked Ned, as he gazed around him.

"It must have been a nice place in its day," returned Joe. "What a pity to let it run down in this fashion."

"The rain is coming around on this side now, Joe; let us shift to the other."

The hermit's boy was willing, and watching their chance, between the downpours, they ran around to another portion of the old lodge.

"It certainly is a little better here," observed Joe, as he dashed the water from his cap.

A minute later the rumbling of the thunder ceased for the time being, and they heard a murmur of voices

Horatio Alger Jr.

coming from one of the rooms of the lodge.

"Why, somebody must be here!" ejaculated Ned. "Who can it be?"

"Two men, by their voices," answered the hermit's boy. "Wait till I take a look at them?"

"Why not go in?" questioned the rich youth, carelessly.

"They may not be persons that we would care to meet, Ned. You know there are some undesirable characters about the lake."

"That's true."

Not far off was a narrow window, the panes of glass of which had long since been broken out. Moving toward this, Joe peered into the apartment beyond.

Close to an old fireplace, in which a few sticks of half-green timber were burning, sat two men. Both were well dressed, and Joe rightfully surmised that they were from the city. Each wore a hunting outfit and had a gun, but neither had any game.

"We came on a wild-goose chase," grumbled one, as he stirred the fire. "Got nothing but a soaking for our pains."

"Never mind, Malone," returned the other, who was evidently the better educated of the two. "As we had to make ourselves scarce in the city this was as good a place to come to as any."

"Don't you think they'll look for us here?"

"Why should they? We were sharp enough not to leave any trail behind - at least, I was."

"Reckon I was just as sharp, Caven."

"You had to be - otherwise you would have been nabbed." Gaff Caven chuckled to himself. "We outwitted them nicely, I must say. We deserve credit."

"I've spent more than half of what I got out of the deal," went on Pat Malone, for such was the full name of one of the speakers.

"I've spent more than that. But never mind, my boy, fortune will favor us again in the near future."

A crash of thunder drowned out the conversation following, and Joe hurried back to where he had left Ned.

"Well, have you found out who they are?" demanded the rich youth, impatiently.

"No, Ned, but I am sure of one thing."

"What is that?"

"They are two bad men."

"What makes you think that?"

"They said something about having to get out of the city, and one spoke about being nabbed. Evidently they went away to avoid arrest."

At this announcement Ned Talmadge whistled softly

to himself.

"Phew! What shall we do about it?" he asked, with a look of concern on his usually passive face.

Joe shrugged his shoulders.

"I don't know what to do."

"Let us listen to what they have to say. Maybe we'll strike some clew to what they have been doing."

"Would that be fair - to play the eaves-dropper?"

"Certainly - if they are evildoers. Anybody who has done wrong ought to be locked up for it," went on Ned boldly.

With caution the two boys made their way to the narrow window, and Ned looked in as Joe had done. The backs of the two men were still towards the opening, so the lads were not discovered.

"What is this new game?" they heard the man called Malone ask, after a peal of thunder had rolled away among the mountains.

"It's the old game of a sick miner with some valuable stocks to sell," answered Gaff Caven.

"Have you got the stocks?"

"To be sure - one thousand shares of the Blue Bell Mine, of Montana, said to be worth exactly fifty thousand dollars."

"Phew! You're flying high, Gaff!" laughed Pat Malone.

"And why not, so long as I sell the stocks?"

"What did they cost you?"

"Well, they didn't cost me fifty thousand dollars," and Gaff Caven closed one eye suggestively.

"You bet they didn't! More than likely they didn't cost you fifty dollars."

"What, such elegantly engraved stocks as those?"

"Pooh! I can buy a bushel-basket full of worthless stocks for a dollar," came from Pat Malone. "But that isn't here nor there. I go into the deal if you give me my fair share of the earnings."

"I'll give you one-third, Pat, and that's a fair share, I think."

"Why not make it half?"

"Because I'll do the most of the work. It's no easy matter to find a victim." And Gaff Caven laughed broadly. He had a good-appearing face, but his eyes were small and not to be trusted.

"All right, I'll go in for a third then. But how soon is the excitement to begin?"

"Oh, in a week or so. I've got the advertisements in the papers already."

"Not in New York?"

Horatio Alger Jr.

"No, it's Philadelphia this time. Perhaps I'll land one of our Quaker friends."

"Don't be so sure. The Quakers may be slow but they generally know what they are doing."

More thunder interrupted the conversation at this point, and when it was resumed the two men talked in such low tones that only an occasional word could be caught by the two boys.

"They surely must be rascals," remarked Ned, in a whisper. "I'm half of a mind to have them locked up."

"That's easier said than done," answered Joe. "Besides, we haven't any positive proofs against them."

The wind was now rising, and it soon blew so furiously that the two boys were forced to seek the shelter of the woodshed, since they did not deem it wise to enter the lodge so long as the two men were inside. They waited in the shed for fully half an hour, when, as suddenly as it had begun, the storm let up and the sun began to peep forth from between the scattering clouds.

"Now we can go home if we wish," said Joe. "But for my part, I'd like to stay and see what those men do, and where they go to."

"Yes, let us stay by all means," answered the rich youth.

They waited a few minutes longer and then Ned suggested that they look into the window of the lodge once more. The hermit's boy was willing, and they approached the larger building with caution.

Much to their astonishment the two strangers had disappeared.

"Hullo! what do you make of that?" cried Ned, in amazement.

"Perhaps they are in one of the other rooms," suggested Joe.

At the risk of being caught, they entered the lodge and looked into one room after another. Every apartment was vacant, and they now saw that the fire in the fireplace had been stamped out.

"They must have left while we were in the woodshed," said Ned.

"Maybe they are out on the lake," answered the hermit's boy, and he ran down to the water's edge, followed by his companion. But though they looked in every direction, not a craft of any kind was to be seen.

"Joe, they didn't take to the water, consequently they must have left by one of the mountain paths."

"That is true, and if they did they'll have no nice time in getting through. All the bushes are sopping wet, and the mud is very slippery in places."

They walked to the rear of the lodge and soon found the footprints of the two strangers. They led through the bushes and were lost at a small brook that ran into the lake.

"There is no use of our trying to follow this any further," said Joe. "You'll get your clothing covered with water and mud."

"I don't intend to follow," answered Ned. "Just the same, I should like to know more about those fellows."

"I wish I had seen their faces."

"Yes, it's a pity we didn't get a better look at them. But I'd know their voices."

By the time they gave up the hunt the sun was shining brightly. Both walked to where the boat had been left, and Joe turned the craft over so that the water might run out. Then he mopped off the seats as best he could.

Ned wanted to go directly home, and he and Joe rowed the craft in the direction of Riverside. As they passed along the lake shore the hermit's boy noted that several trees had been struck by lightning.

"I'm glad the lightning didn't strike the lodge while we were there," said he.

"It was certainly a severe storm while it lasted, Joe. By the way, shall I say anything about those two men?"

"Perhaps it won't do any harm to tell your father, Ned."

"Very well, I'll do it."

Soon Riverside was reached, and having paid for the fish and the outing, Ned Talmadge walked in the direction of his residence. Joe shoved off from the tiny dock and struck out for his home. He did not dream of the calamity that awaited him there.

CHAPTER III.

A HOME IN RUINS.

As Joe rowed toward his home on the mountain side, a good mile from Riverside, he could not help but think of the two mysterious men and of what they had said.

"They were certainly rascals," he mused. "And from their talk they must have come from New York and are now going to try some game in Philadelphia."

The hermit's boy was tired out by the day's outing, yet he pulled a fairly quick stroke and it was not long before he reached the dock at which he and Hiram Bodley were in the habit of leaving their boat. He cleaned the craft out, hid the oars in the usual place, and then, with his fishing lines in one hand and a good sized fish in the other, started up the trail leading to the place that he called home.

"What a place to come to, alongside of the one Ned lives in," he said to himself. "I suppose the Talmadges think this is a regular hovel. I wish we could afford something better, - or at least live in town. It's lonesome here with nobody but old Uncle Hiram around."

As Joe neared the cabin something seemed to come

Horatio Alger Jr.

over him and, for some reason he could not understand, he felt very much depressed in spirits. He quickened his pace, until a turn of the trail brought the homestead into view.

A cry of alarm broke from his lips and with good reason. The little shelter had stood close to a large hemlock tree. The lightning had struck the tree, causing it to topple ever. In falling, it had landed fairly and squarely upon the cabin, smashing it completely. One corner of the cabin was in ashes, but the heavy rain had probably extinguished the conflagration.

"Uncle Hiram!" cried the boy, as soon as he recovered from his amazement. "Uncle Hiram, where are you?"

There was no answer to this call and for the moment Joe's heart seemed to stop beating. Was the old hermit under that pile of ruins? If so it was more than likely he was dead.

Dropping his fish and his lines, the youth sprang to the front of the cabin. The door had fallen to the ground and before him was a mass of wreckage with a small hollow near the bottom. He dropped on his knees and peered inside.

"Uncle Hiram!" he called again.

There was no answer, and he listened with bated breath. Then he fancied he heard a groan, coming from the rear of what was left of the cabin. He ran around to that point and pulled aside some boards and a broken window sash.

"Uncle Hiram, are you here?"

"Joe!" came in a low voice, full of pain. The man tried to say more but could not.

Hauling aside some more boards, Joe now beheld the hermit, lying flat on his back, with a heavy beam resting on his chest. He was also suffering from a cut on the forehead and from a broken ankle.

"This is too bad, Uncle Hiram!" he said, in a trembling voice. "I'll get you out just as soon as I can."

"Be - be careful, Joe - I - I - my ribs must be broken," gasped the hermit.

"I'll be careful," answered the boy, and began to pull aside one board after another. Then he tugged away at the beam but could not budge it.

"Raise it up Joe - it - is - crushing the life ou - out of me," said the hermit faintly.

"I'll pry it up," answered the boy, and ran off to get a block of wood. Then he procured a stout pole and with this raised the heavy beam several inches.

"Can you crawl out, Uncle Hiram?"

There was no answer, and Joe saw that the man had fainted from exhaustion. Fixing the pole so it could not slip, he caught hold of the hermit and dragged him to a place of safety.

Joe had never had to care for a hurt person before and he scarcely knew how to proceed. He laid the hermit on the grass and washed his face with water. Soon Hiram Bodley opened his eyes once more.

Horatio Alger Jr.

"My chest!" he groaned. "All of my ribs must be broken! And my ankle is broken, too!" And he groaned again.

"I had better get a doctor, Uncle Hiram."

"A doctor can't help me."

"Perhaps he can."

"I haven't any faith in doctors. A doctor operated on my mother and killed her."

"But Doctor Gardner is a nice man. He will do all he can for you, I am sure," urged Joe.

"Well, Dr. Gardner is a good fellow I admit. If you - can - can get him - I'll - I'll -" The sufferer tried to go on but could not.

"I think I can get him. But I hate to leave you alone." And Joe stared around helplessly. He wished he had Ned with him.

"Never mind - give me a drink - then go," answered Hiram Bodley. He had often taken Doctor Gardner out to hunt with him and liked the physician not a little.

Inside of five minutes Joe was on the way to the doctor's residence, which was on the outskirts of Riverside. He had left the hermit as comfortable as possible, on a mattress and covered with a cloth to keep off the night air, - for it was now growing late and the sun had set behind the mountains.

Tired though he was the boy pulled with might and

main, and so reached the dock of the physician's home in a short space of time. Running up the walk of the neatly-kept garden, he mounted the piazza and rang the bell several times.

"What's the matter?" asked Doctor Gardner, who came himself to answer the summons.

"Our cabin is in ruins, because of the storm, and Mr. Bodley is badly hurt," answered Joe, and related some of the particulars.

"This is certainly too bad, my boy," said the physician. "I'll come at once and do what I can for him."

He ran for a case of instruments and also for some medicines, and then followed Joe back to the boat.

"You act as if you were tired," said the doctor, after he had watched Joe at the oars for several minutes.

"I am tired, sir - I've been rowing a good deal to-day. But I guess I can make it."

"Let me row," said the physician, and took the oars. He was a fine oarsman, and the trip was made in half the time it would have taken Joe to cover the distance.

At the dock there was a lantern, used by Joe and the hermit when they went fishing at night. This was lit, and the two hurried up the trail to the wreck of the cabin.

Hiram Bodley was resting where Joe had left him. He was breathing with difficulty and did not at first recognize the doctor.

"Take it off!" he murmured. "Take it off! It is - is crushing th - the life out of - of me!"

"Mr. Bodley - Hiram, don't you know me?" asked Doctor Gardner, kindly.

"Oh! So it's you? I guess you can't do much, doctor, can you? I - I'm done for!" And a spasm of pain crossed the sufferer's face.

"While there is life there is hope," answered the physician, noncommittally. He recognized at once that Hiram Bodley's condition was critical.

"He'll get over it, won't he?" questioned Joe, quickly.

The doctor did not answer, but turned to do what he could for the hurt man. He felt of his chest and listened to his breathing, and then administered some medicine.

"His ankle is hurt, too," said Joe.

"Never mind the ankle just now, Joe," was the soft answer.

There was something in the tone that alarmed the boy and he caught the physician by the arm.

"Doctor, tell me the truth!" he cried. "Is he is he going to die?"

"I am afraid so, my lad. His ribs are crushed and one of them has stuck into his right lung."

At these words the tears sprang into the boy's eyes and it was all he could do to keep from crying outright.

Even though the old hermit had been rough in his ways, Joe thought a good deal of the man.

"Cannot you do something, doctor," he pleaded.

"Not here. We might do something in a hospital, but he would not survive the journey. He is growing weaker every moment. Be brave, my lad. It is a terrible trial, I know, but you must remember that all things are for the best."

Joe knelt beside the sufferer and took hold of his hand. Hiram Bodley looked at him and then at the doctor.

"I - I can't live - I know it," he said hoarsely. "Joe, stay by me till I die, won't you?"

"Yes!" faltered the boy. "Oh, this is awful!"

"I'm sorry to leave you so soon, Joe - I - I thought I'd be - be able to do something for you some day."

"You have done something for me, Uncle Hiram."

"All I've got goes to you, Joe. Doctor, do you hear that?"

"I do."

"It - it ain't much, but it's something. The blue box - I put it in the blue box - " Here the sufferer began to cough.

"The blue box?" came from Joe questioningly.

"Yes, Joe, all in the blue box - the papers and the

money - And the blue box is - is -" Again the sufferer began to cough. "I - I want water!" he gasped.

The water was brought and he took a gulp. Then he tried to speak again, but the effort was in vain. The doctor and Joe raised him up.

"Uncle Hiram! Speak to me!" cried the boy.

But Hiram Bodley was past speaking. He had passed to the Great Beyond.

CHAPTER IV.

THE SEARCH FOR THE BLUE BOX.

Three days after his tragic death Hiram Bodley was buried. Although he was fairly well known in the lake region only a handful of people came to his funeral. Joe was the chief mourner, and it can honestly be said that he was much downcast when he followed the hermit to his last resting place.

After the funeral several asked Joe what he intended to do. He could not answer the question.

"Have you found that blue box?" questioned Doctor Gardner.

"No, sir, I have not thought of it."

"Probably it contains money and papers of value, Joe."

"I am going to look for it to-day," said the boy. "I - I couldn't look for it while - while -"

"I understand. Well, I trust you locate the box and that it contains all you hope for," added the physician.

As luck would have it, Ned Talmadge's family had just gone away on a trip to the West, so Mr. Talmadge could offer the boy no assistance. But Ned was on hand and did what he could.

"You don't know what you'll do next, do you, Joe?" asked Ned, as he and Joe returned to the wreck of the cabin.

"No."

"Well, if you haven't any money I'll do what I can for you."

"Thank you, Ned; you are very kind."

"It must be hard to be thrown out on the world in this fashion," went on the rich boy, sympathetically.

"It is hard. After all, I thought a good deal of Uncle Hiram. He was strange in his ways, but he had a good heart."

"Wasn't he shot in the head once by accident in the woods?"

"Yes."

"Maybe that made him queer at times."

"Perhaps so."

"I've got six dollars and a half of my spending money saved up. You may have that if you wish," continued Ned, generously.

"I'd rather not take it, Ned."

"Why not?"

"If I can, I want to be independent. Besides, I think there is money around somewhere," and Joe mentioned the missing blue box.

"You must hunt for that blue box by all means!" cried the rich boy. "I'll help you."

After the death of Hiram Bodley, Joe and two of the lake guides had managed to repair one room of the broken-down cabin, and from this the funeral had taken place.

The room contained a bed, a table, two benches and a few dishes and cooking utensils The floor was bare and the window was broken out. It was truly a most uninviting home.

"Of course you are not going to stay here, now you are alone?" said Ned, after a look around.

"I don't know where else to go, Ned."

"Why not move into town!"

"Perhaps I will. But I want to find that blue box before I decide on anything."

Without delay the two boys set to work among the ruins, looking into every hole and corner they could think of and locate. They pulled away heavy boards and logs, and Joe even got a spade and dug up the ground at certain points.

"It doesn't seem to be here," said Ned, after an hour

had passed.

"It must be here," cried Joe.

"Perhaps it was buried under a tree."

"That may be true. Anyway, I am certain it is somewhere around this cabin."

After that the hunt was continued for another hour, and they visited several spots in that locality where Joe thought the blue box might have been placed. But it was all to no purpose, the box failed to come to light.

At last the two boys sat down on a bench in front of the cabin. Both were tired out, Ned especially so. Joe was much downcast and his friend did what he could to cheer him up.

"The box is bound to come to light some day," said Ned. "That is, unless some of those men carried it off."

"What men, Ned?"

"The fellows who helped to mend the cabin just before the funeral."

"Oh, I don't think they would steal the box. Bart Andrews and Jack Thompson are as honest as the day is long."

"Well, it's mighty queer you can't find some trace of the blue box."

The boys talked the matter over for some time, and then Ned announced that he must go home.

"You can go with me if you wish," he said. "It will be better than staying here all alone."

But Joe declined the offer.

"I'll stay here, and begin the hunt again the first thing in the morning," he said.

"Well, if you want anything, come and see me, Joe; won't you?"

"I will, Ned."

Ned had come over in his own boat and now Joe walked down to the lake with him. His friend gone, the hermit's boy returned to the delapidated cabin.

He was hungry but he had no heart to eat. He munched some bread and cheese which a neighbor had brought over. He felt utterly alone in the great worlds and when he thought of this a strange feeling came over him.

It was a bitter night for the poor boy, but when morning came his mind was made up. He would make his own way in the world, asking aid from no one, not even Ned.

"And if I can't find the blue box I'll get along without it," he told himself.

As soon as it was light he procured breakfast and then started on another hunt for the missing box. The entire day was spent in the search, but without results. Towards night, Joe went down to the lake. Here he caught a couple of small fish, which he fried for his supper.

All told, Joe had exactly a dollar and a half of his own and nine dollars which he had found in the hermit's pocketbook.

"Ten dollars and a half," he mused, as he counted the amount over. "Not very much to go out into the world with. If I want to do anything in town I'll have to buy some clothes."

From this it will be surmised that Joe was thinking of giving up his roving life around the lake and mountains, and this was true.

Hunting and fishing appealed to him only in an uncertain way, and he longed to go forth into the busy world and make something of himself.

He had two suits of clothing, but both were very much worn, and so were his shoes and his cap. Hiram Bodley had left some old clothing, but they were too big for the boy.

"I guess I'll get Jasok the peddler to come up here and make me an offer for what is here," he told himself.

Jasok was a Hebrew peddler who drove around through the lake region, selling tinware and doing all sorts of trading. It was time for him to visit that neighborhood and Joe went to the nearest house on the main road and asked about the man.

"He will most likely be along to-morrow, Joe," said the neighbor.

"If he comes, Mr. Smith, will you send him over to my place? Tell him I want an offer for the things."

"Going to sell out, Joe?"

"Yes, sir."

"What are you going to do after that?"

"Try for some job in town."

"That's a good idea. Hunting and fishing isn't what it used to be. What do you want for the things?"

"All I can get," and a brief smile hovered on Joe's face.

"I wouldn't sell out too cheap. Jasok is a great fellow to drive a bargain."

"If he won't give me a fair price, I'll load the things on the rowboat and sell them in town."

"That's an idea. Do you want to sell Hiram's double-barrel shot gun?"

"Yes, sir."

"I'll give you ten dollars for it."

"I was going to ask twelve, Mr. Smith. It's a pretty good gun."

"So it is, although it is a little bit old-fashioned. Well, bring it over and I'll allow you twelve dollars," answered the neighbor, who was willing to assist Joe all he could.

Joe went back for the gun without delay, and received his money. Then he returned to the cabin and brought out all the goods he wished to sell.

By the middle of the next day the Hebrew peddler appeared. At first he declared that all of the things Joe had to sell were not worth two dollars.

"Very well, if you think that, we won't talk about it," said Joe, briefly.

"Da vos all vorn out," said Jasok. "De clothes vos rags, and de furniture an' dishes was kracked."

"If you don't want them, I'll take them to town and sell them. I am sure Moskowsky will buy them."

Now it happened that Moskowsky was a rival peddler who also boasted of the ownership of a second-hand store. To think that the goods might go to this man nettled Jasok exceedingly.

"Vell, I likes you, Cho," he said. "I vos your friend, an' I gif you dree dollars for dem dings."

"You can have them for ten dollars," answered the boy.

A long talk followed, and in the end the Hebrew peddler agreed to pay seven dollars and a half, providing Joe would help to carry the goods to the main road, where the wagon had been left. The money was paid over, and by nightfall all of the goods were on the wagon, and Joe was left at the cabin with nothing but the suit on his back. But he had thirty dollars in his pocket, which he counted over with great satisfaction.

"I ought to be able to get something to do before that is

gone," he told himself. "If I don't, it will be my own fault."

Horatio Alger Jr.

CHAPTER V.

A NEW SUIT OF CLOTHES.

On the following day it rained early in the morning, so Joe had to wait until noon before he left the old cabin. He took with him all that remained of his possessions, including the precious pocketbook with the thirty dollars. When he thought of the blue box he sighed.

"Perhaps it will never come to light," he told himself. "Well, if it does not I'll have to make the best of it."

Two o'clock found him on the streets of Riverside, which was a town of fair size. During the summer months many visitors were in the place and the hotels and boarding houses were crowded.

There was one very fine clothing store in Riverside, but Joe did not deem it best, with his limited capital, to go there for a suit. Instead he sought out a modest establishment on one of the side streets.

Just ahead of him was an Irish couple who had evidently not been in this country many years. The man entered the store awkwardly, as if he did not feel at home. Not so his wife, who walked a little in advance of her husband.

"Have you got any men's coats?" said she to the clerk who came forward to wait on the pair. "If I can get one cheap for me husband here I'll buy one."

"Oh, yes, madam," was the ready reply. "We have the best stock in town, by all odds. You can't fail to be suited."

So saying, he led the way to a counter piled high with the articles called for, and hauled them over.

"There," said he, pulling out one of a decidedly ugly pattern. "There is one of first quality cloth. It was made for a gentleman of this town, but did not exactly fit him, and so we'll sell it cheap."

"And what is the price?"

"Three dollars."

"Three dollars!" exclaimed the Irish lady, lifting up her hands in extreme astonishment.

"Three dollars! You'll be afther thinkin' we're made of money, sure! I'll give you a dollar and a half."

"No, ma'am, we don't trade in that way. We don't very often take half what we ask for an article."

"Mike," said she, "pull off yer coat an' thry it on. Three dollars, and it looks as if it was all cotton."

"Not a thread of cotton in that," was the clerk's reply.

"Not wan, but a good many, I'm thinkin'," retorted the Irish lady, as she helped her husband draw on the coat.

It fitted tolerably well and Mike seemed mightily pleased with his transformation.

"Come," said the wife. "What will ye take?"

"As it's you, I'll take off twenty-five cents," replied the clerk.

"And sell it to me for two dollars?" inquired his customer, who had good cause for her inaccurate arithmetic.

"For two dollars and seventy-five cents."

"Two dollars and seventy-five cents! It's taking the bread out of the childer's mouths you'd have us, paying such a price as that! I'll give you two twenty-five, an' I'll be coming again some time."

"We couldn't take so low as two twenty- five, ma'am. You may have it for two dollars and a half."

After another ineffectual attempt to get it for two dollars and a quarter, the Irish woman finally offered two dollars and forty-five cents, and this offer was accepted.

She pulled out a paper of change and counted out two dollars and forty cents, when she declared that she had not another cent. But the clerk understood her game and coolly proceeded to put the coat back on the pile. Then the woman very opportunely found another five-cent piece stored away in the corner of her pocket.

"It's robbin' me, ye are," said she as she paid it over.

"Oh, no, ma'am, you are getting a great bargain," answered the clerk.

Joe had witnessed the bargaining with a good deal of quiet amusement. As soon as the Irish couple had gone the clerk came toward the boy.

"Well, young man, what can I do for you?" he asked, pleasantly.

"I want a suit of clothing. Not an expensive suit, but one guaranteed to be all wool."

"A light or a dark suit?"

"A dark gray."

"I can fit you out in a fine suit of this order," and the clerk pointed to several lying in a heap nearby.

"I don't want that sort. I want something on the order of those in the window marked nine dollars and a half."

"Oh, all right."

Several suits were brought forth, and one was found that fitted Joe exceedingly well.

"You guarantee this to be all wool?" asked the boy.

"Every thread of it."

"Then I'll take it"

"Very well; the price is twelve dollars."

"Isn't it like that in the window?"

"On that order, but a trifle better."

"It seems to me to be about the same suit. I'll give you nine dollars and a half."

"I can't take it. I'll give it to you for eleven and a half. That is our best figure."

"Then I'll go elsewhere for a suit," answered Joe, and started to leave the clothing establishment.

"Hold on, don't be so fast!" cried the clerk, catching him by the arm. "I'll make it eleven and a quarter."

"Not a cent more than the advertised price, nine and a half," replied Joe, firmly.

"Oh, but this isn't the same suit."

"It's just like it, to my eye. But you needn't sell it for that if you don't want it. Mason & Harris are offering some bargains, I believe."

"You can get a better bargain here than anywhere in this town, or in Philadelphia either," answered the clerk, who did not intend to let his prospective customer get away. "We'll make it an even eleven dollars and say no more about it."

Instead of answering Joe started once more for the door.

"Hold on!"

"I haven't got time."

"Make it ten and a half. At that price we are losing exactly half a dollar on that suit."

"Not a cent over what I offered."

"We can't sell suits at such a loss. It would ruin us."

"Then don't do it. I think Mason & Harris have some good suits very cheap. And they are quite up-to-date, too," added Joe.

"Our suits are the best in town, young man. Take this one for an even ten dollar bill."

"I will if you'll throw in one of those half dollar caps," answered our hero.

"Well, have your own way, but it's a sacrifice," grumbled the clerk.

He wanted to wrap up the suit, but, afraid he might substitute something else, Joe insisted upon donning the suit then and there and likewise the new cap. Then he had the old articles of wearing apparel done up into a bundle and paid over the ten dollars.

"You're pretty smart after a bargain," said the clerk.

"I've got to be - when I strike such fellows as you," was the reply.

"You got a better bargain than that Irish woman did."

"I did - if the suit is all wool. But if it's cotton, I'm

stuck," returned our hero, and with his bundle under his arm he walked from the store.

He had left his rowboat in charge of an old boatman named Ike Fairfield, and now he walked down to the boathouse.

"Just in time, Joe," said the old boatman. "Want to earn a dollar?"

"To be sure I do," answered our hero.

"A party of ladies want a long row around the lake. You can have the job."

"All right, Ike."

"I charged them a dollar and a quarter. I'll keep the quarter for my commission."

"That is fair."

"One of the ladies said she wanted somebody that looked pretty decent. I think you'll fill the bill with that new suit."

"I didn't expect to wear the suit out on the lake, but in this case I'll keep it on," answered Joe.

"I find it pays to keep well dressed, when you take out the summer boarders," answered the old boatman. "And it pays to keep the boats in good shape, too."

"Where am I to get the party?"

"Over to the dock of Mallison's Hotel. One of the

ladies is Mallison's niece."

"Why don't they take a hotel boat?"

"All engaged, two days ago. It's a busy season. But I've got to be going. You had better go over to the dock at once. They want to go out at three o'clock sharp."

"Very well, I'll be on hand," answered our hero.

CHAPTER VI.

AN ACCIDENT ON THE LAKE.

Joe certainly presented a neat appearance when he rowed over to the hotel dock. Before going he purchased a new collar and a dark blue tie, and these, with his new suit and new cap, set him off very well.

The boat had been cleaned in the morning, and when the ladies appeared they inspected the craft with satisfaction.

"What a nice clean boat," said Mabel Mallison, the niece of the proprietor of the hotel.

"And a nice clean boatman, too," whispered one of her friends. "I couldn't bear that man we had day before yesterday, with his dirty hands and the tobacco juice around his mouth."

The ladies to go out were four in number, and two sat in the bow and two in the stern. It made quite a heavy load, but as they were not out for speed our hero did not mind it.

"We wish to go up to Fern Rock," said Mabel Mallison. "They tell me there are some beautiful ferns to be gathered there."

"There are," answered Joe. "I saw them last week."

"And I wish to get some nice birch bark if I can," said another of the ladies.

"I can get you plenty of it."

Joe rowed along in his best style, and while doing so the ladies of the party asked him numerous questions concerning the lake and vicinity. When Fern Rock was reached, all went ashore, and our hero pointed out the ferns he had seen, and dug up such as the others wished to take along. An hour was spent over the ferns, and in getting some birch bark, and then they started on the return for the hotel.

"I'd like to row," cried one of the ladies, a rather plump personage.

"Oh, Jennie, I don't think you can!" cried another.

"Of course I can," answered Jennie, and sprang up from her seat to take the oars.

"Be careful!" came in a warning from Joe, as the boat began to rock.

"Oh, I'm not afraid!" said the plump young lady, and leaned forward to catch hold of one oar. Just then her foot slipped and she fell on the gunwale, causing the boat to tip more than ever. As she did this, Mabel Mallison, who was leaning over the side, gazing down into the clear waters of the lake, gave a shriek.

"Oh, save me!" came from her, and then she went over, with a loud splash.

Joe was startled, and the ladies left in the boat set up a wail of terror.

"She will be drowned!"

"Oh, save her! Save her, somebody!"

"It is my fault!" shrieked the plump young lady. "I tipped the boat over!"

Joe said nothing, but looked over the side of the boat. He saw the body of Mabel Mallison not far away. But it was at the lake bottom and did not offer to rise.

"It's queer she doesn't come up," he thought.

Then he gave a second look and saw that the dress of the unfortunate one was caught in some sharp rocks. Without hesitation he dived overboard, straight for the bottom.

It was no easy matter to unfasten the garment, which was caught in a crack between two heavy stones. But at the second tug it came free, and a moment later both our hero and Mabel Mallison came to the surface.

"Oh!" cried two of the ladies in the row-boat. "Is she drowned?"

"I trust not," answered Joe. "Sit still, please, or the boat will surely go over."

As best he could Joe hoisted Mabel into the craft and then clambered in himself. As he did so the unfortunate girl gave a gasp and opened her eyes.

"Oh!" she murmured.

"You are safe now, Mabel!" said one of her companions.

"And to think it was my fault!" murmured the plump young lady. "I shall never forgive myself as long as I live!"

Mabel Mallison had swallowed some water, but otherwise she was unhurt. But her pretty blue dress was about ruined, and Joe's new suit did not look near as well as it had when he had donned it.

"Let us row for the hotel," said one of the young ladies. "Are you all right?" she asked of Joe.

"Yes, ma'am, barring the wetting."

"It was brave of you to go down after Mabel."

"Indeed it was!" cried that young lady. "If it hadn't been for you I might have been drowned." And she gave a deep shudder.

"I saw she was caught and that's why I went over after her," answered our hero simply. "It wasn't so much to do."

All dripping as he was, Joe caught up the oars of the boat and sent the craft in the direction of the hotel at a good speed. That she might not take cold, a shawl was thrown over Mabel's wet shoulders.

The arrival of the party at the hotel caused a mild sensation. Mabel hurried to her room to put on dry clothing, and Joe was directed to go around to the kitchen. But when the proprietor of the place had heard what Joe had done for his niece he sent the lad to a private apartment and provided him with dry clothing belonging to another who was of our hero's size.

"That was a fine thing to do, young man," said the hotel proprietor, when Joe appeared, dressed in the dry garments, and his own clothing had been sent to the laundry to be dried and pressed.

"I'm glad I was there to do it, Mr. Mallison."

"Let me see, aren't you Hiram Bodley's boy?"

"I lived with Mr. Bodley, yes."

"That is what I mean. It was a terrible accident that killed him. Are you still living at the tumbled-down cabin?"

"No, sir. I've just sold off the things, and I am going to settle in town."

"Where?"

"I haven't decided that yet. I was going to hunt up a place when Ike Fairfield gave me the job of rowing out the young ladies."

"I see. You own the boat, eh?"

"Yes, sir."

"You ought to be able to make a fair living, taking out summer boarders."

"I suppose so, but that won't give me anything to do this winter."

"Well, perhaps something else will turn up by that time." Andrew Mallison drew out a fat wallet. "I want to reward you for saving Mabel."

He drew out two ten-dollar bills and held them towards our hero. But Joe shook his head and drew back.

"Thank you very much, Mr. Mallison, but I don't want any reward."

"But you have earned it fairly, my lad."

"I won't touch it. If you want to help me you can throw some odd rowing jobs from the hotel in my way."

"Then you won't really touch the money?"

"No, sir."

"How would you like to work for the hotel regularly?"

"I'd like it first-rate if it paid."

"I can guarantee you regular work so long as the summer season lasts."

"And what would it pay?"

"At least a dollar a day, and your board."

"Then I'll accept and with thanks for your kindness."

"When can you come?"

"I'm here already."

"That means that you can stay from now on?"

"Yes, sir."

"I don't suppose you want the job of hauling somebody from the lake every day," said Andrew Mallison, with a smile.

"Not unless I was dressed for it, Mr. Mallison. Still, it has been the means of getting me a good position."

"I shall feel safe in sending out parties with you for I know you will do your best to keep them from harm."

"I'll certainly do that, I can promise you."

"To-morrow you can take out two old ladies who wish to be rowed around the whole lake and shown every point of interest. Of course you know all the points."

"Yes, sir, I know every foot of ground around the lake, and I know the mountains, too."

"Then there will be no difficulty in keeping you busy. I am glad to take you on. I am short one man - or will be by to-night. I am going to let Sam Cullum go, for he drinks too much."

"Well, you won't have any trouble with me on that score."

"Don't you drink?"

"Not a drop, sir."

"I am glad to hear it, and it is to your credit," concluded the hotel proprietor.

CHAPTER VII.

BLOWS AND KIND DEEDS.

Several days passed and Joe went out half a dozen times on the lake with parties from the hotel. All whom he served were pleased with him and treated him so nicely that, for the time being, his past troubles were forgotten.

At the beginning of the week Ned Talmadge came to see him.

"I am going away to join the folks out West," said Ned.

"I hope you will have a good time," answered our hero.

"Oh, I'm sure to have that, Joe. By the way, you are nicely settled here, it would seem."

"Yes, and I am thankful for it."

"Mr. Mallison is a fine man to work for, so I have been told. You had better stick to him."

"I shall - as long as the work holds out."

"Maybe he will give you something else to do, after the boating season is over."

A few more words passed, and then Ned took his departure. It was to be a long time before the two friends would meet again.

So far Joe had had no trouble with anybody around the hotel, but that evening, when he was cleaning out his boat, a man approached him and caught him rudely by the shoulder.

"So you're the feller that's took my job from me, eh?" snarled the newcomer.

Our hero looked up and recognized Sam Cullum, the boatman who had been discharged for drinking. Even now the boatman was more than half under the influence of intoxicants.

"I haven't taken anybody's job from him," answered Joe.

"I say yer did!" growled Cullum. "It ain't fair, nuther!"

To this our hero did not reply, but went on cleaning out his boat.

"Fer two pins I'd lick yer!" went on the tipsy boatman, lurching forward.

"See here, Sam Cullum, I want you to keep your distance," said Joe, sharply. "Mr. Mallison discharged you for drinking. I had nothing to do with it."

"I don't drink; leastwise, I don't drink no more'n I need."

"Yes, you do. It would be the best thing in the world

for you if you'd leave liquor alone entirely."

"Humph! don't you preach to me, you little imp!"

"Then leave me alone."

"You stole the job from me an' I'm going to lick you for it."

"If you touch me you'll get hurt," said Joe, his eyes flashing. "Leave me alone and I'll leave you alone."

"Bah!" snarled the other, and struck out awkwardly. He wanted to hit Joe on the nose, but the boy dodged with ease, and Sam Cullum fell sprawling over the rowboat.

"Hi! what did ye trip me up for?" spluttered the half-intoxicated man, as he rose slowly. "Don't you do that ag'in, do yer hear?"

"Then don't try to strike me again."

There was a moment of silence and then Sam Cullum gathered himself for another blow. By this time a small crowd of boys and hotel helpers began to collect.

"Sam Cullum's going to fight Joe Bodley!"

"Sam'll most kill Joe!"

With all his strength the man rushed at Joe. But the boy dodged again and put out his foot and the man went headlong.

"Now will you let me alone?" asked our hero, coolly.

"No, I won't!" roared Sam Cullum. "Somebody give me a club! I'll show him!"

Arising once more, he caught up an oar and launched a heavy blow at Joe's head. For a third time our hero dodged, but the oar struck him on the arm, and the blow hurt not a little.

Joe was now angry and believed it was time to defend himself. He edged towards the end of the dock and Sam Cullum followed. Then, of a sudden the boy ducked under the man's arm, turned, and gave him a quick shove that sent him with a splash into the lake.

"Hurrah! score one for Joe!"

"That will cool Sam Cullum's temper."

"Yes, and perhaps it will sober him a little," came from a man standing by, who had witnessed the quarrel from the beginning. "He brought this on himself; the boy had nothing to do with it."

Sam Cullum floundered around in the water like a whale cast up in the shallows. The lake at that point was not over four feet deep, but he did not know enough to stand upright.

"Save me!" he bellowed. "Save me! I don't want to drown!"

"Swallow a little water, it will do you good!" said a bystander, with a laugh.

"Walk out and you'll be all right," added another.

At last Sam Cullum found his feet and walked around the side of the dock to the shore. A crowd followed him and kept him from going at Joe again.

"I'll fix him another time," growled the intoxicated one, and shuffled off, with some small boys jeering him.

"You treated him as he deserved," said one of the other boatmen to Joe.

"I suppose he'll try to square up another time," answered our hero.

"Well, I wouldn't take water for him, Joe."

"I don't intend to. If he attacks me I'll do the best I can to defend myself."

"He has made a nuisance of himself for a long time. It's a wonder to me that Mr. Mallison put up with it so long."

"He was short of help, that's why. It isn't so easy to get new help in the height of the summer season."

"That is true."

Joe expected to have more trouble with Sam Cullum the next day but it did not come. Then it leaked out that Cullum had gotten into a row with his wife and some of her relatives that night and was under arrest. When the boatman was brought up for trial the Judge sentenced him to six months' imprisonment.

"And it serves him right," said the man who brought

the news to Joe.

"It must be hard on his wife."

"Well, it is, Joe."

"Have they any children?"

"Four - a boy of seven and three little girls."

"Are they well off?"

"What, with such a father? No, they are very poor. She used to go out washing, but now she has to stay at home to take care of the baby. Sam was a brute to strike her. I don't wonder the relatives took a hand."

"Perhaps the relatives can help her."

"They can't do much, for they are all as poor as she is, and one of them is just getting over an operation at the hospital."

"Where do the Cullums live?"

"Down on Railroad Alley, not far from the water tower. It's a mite of a cottage."

Joe said no more, but what he had been told him set him to thinking, and that evening, after his work was over, he took a walk through the town and in the direction of Railroad Alley.

Not far from the water station he found the Cullum homestead, a mite of a cottage, as the man had said, with a tumbled-down chimney and several broken-out windows. He looked in at one of the windows and by the light of a smoking kerosene lamp beheld a woman in a rocking-chair, rocking a baby to sleep. Three other youngsters were standing around, knowing not what to do. On a table were some dishes, all bare of food.

"Mamma, I want more bread," one of the little ones was saying.

"You can have more in the morning, Johnny," answered the mother.

"No, I want it now," whimpered the youngster. "I'm hungry."

"I'm hungry, too," put in another little one.

"I can't give you any more to-night, for I haven't it," said the mother, with a deep sigh. "Now, be still, or you'll wake the baby."

"Why don't dad come home?" asked the boy of seven.

"He can't come home, Bobby - he - had to go away," faltered the mother. "Now all be still, and you shall have more bread in the morning."

The children began to cry, and unable to stand the sight any longer Joe withdrew. Up the Alley was a grocery store and he almost ran to this.

"Give me some bread," he said, "and some cake, and a pound of cheese, and some smoked beef, and a pound of good tea, and some sugar. Be quick, please."

The goods were weighed out and wrapped up, and with

his arms full he ran back to the cottage and kicked on the door.

"Who is there?" asked Mrs. Cullum, in alarm.

"Here are some groceries for you!" cried Joe. "All paid for!"

"Oh, look!" screamed the boy of seven. "Bread, and cheese!"

"And sugar!" came from one of the little girls.

"And tea! Mamma, just what you like!" said another.

"Where did this come from?" asked Mrs. Cullum.

"A friend," answered Joe. "It's all paid for."

"I am very thankful."

"Now we can have some bread, can't we?" queried the boy.

"Yes, and a bit of smoked beef and cheese, too," said the mother, and placing the sleeping baby on a bed, she proceeded to deal out the good things to her children.

CHAPTER VIII.

THE TIMID MR. GUSSING.

It was not until the children had been satisfied and put to bed that Joe had a chance to talk to Mrs. Cullum. She was greatly astonished when she learned who he was.

"I didn't expect this kindness," said she. "I understand that my husband treated you shamefully."

"It was the liquor made him do it ma'am," answered our hero. "I think he'd be all right if he'd leave drink alone."

"Yes, I am sure of it!" She gave a long sigh. "He was very kind and true when we were first married. But then he got to using liquor and - and - this is the result."

"Perhaps he will turn over a new leaf when he comes out of jail."

"I hope he does. If he doesn't, I don't know what I am going to do."

"Have you anything to do?"

"I used to wash for two families in town but they have regular hired help now."

"Perhaps you can get more work, if you advertise. If you'll allow me, I'll put an advertisement in the Riverside News for you."

"Thank you. I don't see what makes you so kind."

"Well, I have been down in the world myself, Mrs. Cullum, so I know how to feel for others."

"Did you say you used to live with Bodley, the hermit?"

"Yes."

"My folks used to know him. He was rather a strange man after he got shot by accident."

"Yes, but he was kind."

"Are you his son?"

"No. He said I was his nephew. But I never found out much about that."

"Oh, yes, I remember something about that. He had a brother who lost his wife and several children. Are you that man's son?"

"I believe I am."

"And you have never heard from your father?"

"Not a word."

"That is hard on you."

"I am going to look for my father some day."

"If so, I hope you will find him."

"So do I." Joe arose. "I must be going." He paused. "Mrs. Cullum, will you let me help you?" he added, earnestly.

"Why, you have helped me a good deal already. Not one in a thousand would do what you have done - after the way my husband treated you."

"I thought that you might be short of money."

"I must confess I am."

"I am not rich but, if you can use it, I can let you have five dollars."

"I'll accept it as a loan. I don't want you to give me the money," answered the poor woman. She thought of the things she absolutely needed, now that her husband was gone.

The money was handed over, and a few minutes later Joe took his departure. Somehow his heart felt very light because of his generosity. He had certainly played the part of a friend in need.

But he did not stop there. Early in the morning he sought out Andrew Mallison and told the hotel proprietor of Mrs. Cullum's condition.

"I was thinking that you might be able to give her work

in the hotel laundry," he continued.

The hotel man called up the housekeeper and from her learned that another woman could be used to iron.

"You can let her come and we'll give her a trial," said he.

It did not take Joe long to communicate with the poor woman, and she was overjoyed to see work in sight, without waiting for an advertisement in the newspaper.

"I'll go at once," said she. "I'll get a neighbor's girl to mind the children." And she was as good as her word. As it happened, she proved to be a good laundress, and Mr. Mallison gave her steady employment until her husband came from jail. Then, much to his wife's satisfaction, Sam Cullum turned over a new leaf and became quite sober and industrious.

Joe was now becoming well acquainted around the hotel and took an interest in many of the boarders.

Among the number was a young man named Felix Gussing. He was a nice individual in his way, but had certain peculiarities. One was that he was exceedingly afraid of horses and at every possible opportunity he gave them as wide a berth as possible.

"Don't like them at all, don't you know," he said, to Joe, during a boat ride. "Can't understand them at all."

"Oh, I think a good horse is very nice," answered our hero.

"But they are so - so balkish - so full of kicking,"

insisted Felix Gussing.

"Well, I admit some of them are," answered Joe.

There were two young ladies stopping at the hotel and the young man had become quite well acquainted with both of them. One he thought was very beautiful and was half tempted to propose to her.

On the day after the boat ride with Joe, Felix Gussing took the ladies to have some ice cream, and during the conversation all spoke of a certain landmark of interest located about three miles from Riverside.

"I have seen it and it is - aw - very interesting," drawled Felix.

"Then we must see it, Belle," said one of the young ladies, to her companion.

"Oh, I'm not going to walk that far," answered Belle, with a bewitching look at the young man.

"You might drive over," suggested Felix, without stopping to think twice.

"Oh, yes, I love driving!" cried one of the girls.

"And so do I!" answered the other.

"I will find out what can be done about a conveyance," answered Felix.

Being a good deal of a dude, and dressing very fastidiously, he did not much relish visiting the livery stable attached to the hotel. But, early on the following morning, he walked down to the place, and ordered a horse and carriage, to be ready at ten o'clock.

Now it must be known that Felix did not intend to drive the carriage. He thought the young ladies would drive for themselves, since both had said that they loved driving. Unfortunate man! he knew not the snare he had laid for himself!

Punctual to the minute the carriage drove up to the door.

Felix was on hand, standing on the steps, with politeness in his air, though with trembling in his heart because so near the horses. He assisted the ladies in. Then he handed the reins to Miss Belle.

"Do you wish me to hold the horses while you get in?" she asked sweetly.

"Till I get in!" ejaculated Felix, taken aback.

"Certainly! You don't think we are going to drive ourselves, do you? Of course you are going with us."

Poor Felix! He was "in for it" now, decidedly. It required a good deal of moral courage, a quality in which he was deficient, to resist a lady's demand. His knees trembled with fear as he scrambled in. Joe, who was standing not far away, looked on with a quiet smile on his face. He realized what was passing in the dude's mind.

"He'd give ten dollars to get out of it," our hero told himself.

The boy who had brought the turnout around looked at Felix Gussing earnestly.

"Take care of that horse, mister," said he, warningly. "He's young and a little bit wild."

"Wild?" gasped the dude. "I - I don't want to drive a wild horse."

"Oh, he'll be all right if you keep an eye on him," went on the stable boy.

"Young and a little bit wild!" thought Felix to himself. "Oh, dear, what in the world shall I do? I never drove a horse before. If I get back with less than a broken neck I'll be lucky! I'd give a thousand to be out of this pickle."

"Hadn't we better start, Mr. Gussing?" asked one of the young ladies, after a pause.

"Oh, yes - certainly!" he stammered. "But - er - you can drive if you wish."

"Thank you, but I would prefer that you drive."

"Won't you drive?" he asked of the other young lady.

"Oh, no, not to-day. But I'll use the whip if you say so," she answered.

"Not for the world!" cried the unhappy Felix. "He is a bit wild already and there is no telling what he'd do if he felt the whip."

At last the carriage drove off. Joe gazed after it thoughtfully.

"Unless I miss my guess, there is going to be trouble before that drive is over," he thought. And there was trouble, as we shall soon learn.

CHAPTER IX.

AN UNFORTUNATE OUTING.

Fortunately for the unhappy Felix the horse walked away from the hotel in an orderly fashion, and soon they gained the highway leading to the resort the party wished to visit.

Had the dude left the horse alone all might have gone well. But he deemed it necessary to pull on first one line and then the other, which kept the carriage in a meandering course.

"I don't think, Mr. Gussing, that you can be much used to driving," said one of the young ladies, presently.

"That's a fact," answered the dude.

"Why don't you keep to the right of the road?"

"Well, - er - the fact is, this horse is a very difficult one to drive. I don't believe I ever drove one which was more so."

As this was the first horse Mr. Gussing had ever driven, this assertion was true in every particular.

"Oh, I can't travel so slow!" cried one of the young

ladies, and seized the whip, and before Felix could stop her, used it on the steed.

The effect was magical. The horse started up like a racer, and tore through the street as if trying to win a race for a thousand dollars.

The dude clung to the reins in the wildest terror. To his frenzied imagination it seemed that his final hour was approaching.

"Whoa!" he screamed, jerking on the lines. "Stop, you crazy beast! Stop, before we all get killed!"

But the horse only went the faster. And now, to increase his alarm, he saw a buggy approaching from the opposite direction. It contained one of the town lawyers, Silas Simms by name.

"We shall run into that buggy!" screamed the fair Belle. "Oh, Mr. Gussing, be careful!"

A moment later the two turnouts came together with a crash, and one wheel was torn from the buggy and the town lawyer pitched out headlong to the ground. Then on went the carriage with the dude and the two young ladies, at a faster pace than ever.

"Let me jump out!" screamed one of the ladies.

"No, not yet! You'll be killed, Grace," answered Belle.

"Then stop the carriage!"

Alas, the poor Felix was already doing his best to stop the horse. But his jerkings on the reins only added to the horse's wildness.

Not far along the road was a good sized brook, spanned by a neat wooden bridge. As the carriage neared the bridge, Felix pulled on the wrong rein once again. The horse turned from the road proper, and descended full speed into the stream itself.

"Oh, now we'll be drowned!" shrieked Grace.

But she was mistaken. The stream was easily fordable, so there was no danger on that score. But the rate at which they were impelled through the water naturally created no inconsiderable splashing, so that on emerging on the other side the dude, as well as the young ladies, were well drenched.

To the great joy of Felix the contact with the water cooled the ardor of the steed, so that he resumed the journey at a far more moderate rate of speed.

"Wasn't it just glorious!" cried Belle, who, after the danger seemed past, grew enthusiastic. "What a noble animal!"

"Glorious?" echoed the dude. "I don't care much about such glory. As for the noble animal - I - er - I wish he was hung! That's the best he deserves."

The dude spoke bitterly, for the spell of terror was still on him. Had he consulted his own wishes he would have leaped from the carriage and left the ladies to their fate.

But the thought of the bewitching Belle made him keep his seat, and he resolved that if he must die he would do it like a martyr.

The horse went on, and at last they neared the end of the short journey. But here a new obstacle presented itself. There was a big fence and a gate, and the gate was tight shut.

As they could not enter the grounds without opening the gate, the dude got down out of the carriage. He did not hand the reins to either of the ladies but laid them over the dashboard.

The instant the gate was swung open the steed darted forward, and brought up with a jerk against a post that happened to be in the way. Here he reared and plunged, causing the young ladies to scream "murder" at the top of their voices.

"Oh, my! Oh, dear me!" bawled Felix, and took refuge behind a neighboring hedge. "The horse has gone crazy! He'll bite somebody next!"

The cries reached some men who were not far off, and they came running to the assistance of the party. One caught the steed by the bridle and soon had him quieted down.

"I'll never drive that horse again!" said the dude. "Not for a million dollars!"

"How are we to get home?" queried Belle.

"I'll drive you," said one of the men. "I know this horse. He used to belong to Bill Perkins. I know how to handle him."

"Then do so," answered Felix, "and I'll pay you two dollars."

The man was as good as his word, and to Felix's astonishment he made the horse go back to the hotel without the slightest mishap. Then the horse was put in the stable, the dude paid the bill, and the party separated.

"I shall never drive again, never!" declared the dude to himself, and it may be added that he kept his word.

"I hope you had a nice drive," said Joe, when he met Felix that evening.

"It was beastly, don't you know," was the answer. "That horse was a terribly vicious creature."

"He looked to be gentle enough when he started off."

"I think he is a crazy horse."

"By the way, Mr. Gussing, Mr. Silas Simms was looking for you."

"You mean that lawyer who drives the spotted white horse?"

"Yes."

Felix gave a groan.

"He says he wants damages."

"It wasn't my fault that the horse ran into him."

"Well, he is very angry about it, anyway," said our hero.

Early the next morning Felix Gussing received a communication from the lawyer. It was in the following terms: -

"MR. GUSSING. Sir: - In consequence of your reckless driving yesterday, I was thrown from my carriage, receiving a contusion on my shoulder and other injuries. My carriage was also nearly ruined. If you choose to make a race-course of the public highways you must abide the consequences. The damage I have sustained I cannot estimate at less than one hundred and fifty dollars. Indemnify me for that and I will go no further. Otherwise, I shall be compelled to resort to legal action.

"SILAS SIMMS, Atty.

Felix read the letter several times and his knees shook visibly. He did not want to pay over such an amount, yet it struck him with terror when he thought he might possibly be arrested for fast driving. He went to see Mr. Silas Simms.

"I am very sorry," he began.

"Have you come to pay?" demanded the attorney, curtly.

"Well - er - the fact is - don't you think you are asking rather a stiff price, Mr. Simms?"

"Not at all! Not at all, sir! I ought to have placed the damages at three hundred!"

"I'll give you fifty dollars and call it square."

"No, sir, a hundred and fifty! Not a penny less, not one penny! Look at my nose, sir - all scratched! And my ear! Not a penny less than one hundred and fifty dollars!" And the lawyer pounded on his desk with his fist.

"All right then, I'll pay you, but you must give me a receipt in full," answered the dude.

He had to wait until the bank opened, that he might cash a check, and then he paid over the amount demanded. The lawyer drew up a legal paper discharging him from all further obligations. Felix read it with care and stowed it in his pocket.

"And now let me give you some advice, Mr. Gussing," said the lawyer, after the transaction was concluded. "Don't drive such a wild horse again."

"Depend upon it, I never shall," answered the dude. "It costs too much!" he added, with a faint smile.

"Are you well acquainted with horses?"

"No."

"Then you had better leave them alone altogether."

"I have already made up my mind to do so."

CHAPTER X.

DAVID BALL FROM MONTANA.

Finding that Joe could be depended upon, Mr. Mallison put him in charge of all of the boats at the hotel, so that our hero had almost as much work ashore as on the lake.

During the week following, the events just narrated, many visitors left the hotel and others came in. Among those to go were Felix Gussing and the two young ladies. The dude bid our hero a cordial good-bye, for he now knew Joe quite well.

"Good-bye, Mr. Gussing," said Joe. "I hope we meet again."

"Perhaps we shall, although I generally go to a different place each summer."

"Well, I don't expect to stay in Riverside all my life."

"I see. If you make a move, I hope you do well," returned Felix.

On the day after the dude left, a man came to the hotel who, somehow, looked familiar to our hero. He came dressed in a light overcoat and a slouch hat, and carried

Horatio Alger Jr.

a valise and a suit case.

"I've seen him before, but where?" Joe asked himself not once but several times.

The man registered as David Ball, and put down his address as Butte, Montana. He said he was a mining expert, but added that he was sick and the doctors had ordered him to come East for a rest.

"'ve heard of Riverside being a nice place," said he, "so I came on right after striking Pittsburg."

"We shall do all we can to make your stay a pleasant one," said the hotel proprietor, politely.

"All I want is a nice sunny room, where I can get fresh air and take it easy," said the man.

He was willing to pay a good price, and so obtained one of the best rooms in the house, one overlooking the river and the lake. He ate one meal in the dining room, but after that he had his meals sent to his apartment.

"Is he sick?" asked Joe, after watching the man one day.

"He certainly doesn't seem to be well," answered Andrew Mallison.

"It runs in my mind that I have seen him before, but I can't place him," went on our hero.

"You must be mistaken, Joe. I questioned him and he says this is his first trip to the East, although he has frequently visited St. Louis and Chicago."

On the following day the man called for a physician and Doctor Gardner was sent for.

"I've got pains here," said the man from the West, and pointed to his chest. "Do you think I am getting consumption?"

The Riverside physician made a careful examination and then said the man had probably strained himself.

"Reckon I did," was the ready answer. "I was in the mine and a big rock came down on me. I had to hold it up for ten minutes before anybody came to my aid. I thought I was a dead one sure."

"I will give you some medicine and a liniment," said the doctor. "Perhaps you'll feel better after a good rest." And then he left.

That afternoon Joe had to go up into the hotel for something and passed the room of the new boarder. He saw the man standing by the window, gazing out on the water.

"I'm dead certain I've seen him before," mused our hero. "It is queer I can't think where."

Doctor Gardner wanted to be taken across the lake and Joe himself did the job. As he was rowing he asked about the man who had signed the hotel register as David Ball from Montana."

"Is he very sick, doctor?"

"No, I can't say that he is," was the physician's answer. "He looks to be as healthy as you or I."

"It's queer he keeps to his room."

"Perhaps something happened out at his mine to unsettle his nerves. He told me of some sort of an accident."

"Is he a miner?"

"He is a mine owner, so Mr. Mallison told me, but he never heard of the man before."

The stranger received several letters the next day and then a telegram. Shortly after that he took to his bed.

"I am feeling worse," said he to the bell boy who answered his ring. "I want you to send for that doctor again. Ask him to call about noon."

"Yes, sir," answered the boy, and Doctor Gardner was sent for without delay. He came and made another examination and left some medicine.

"I'll take the medicine regularly," said the stranger, who was in bed. But when the doctor had left he quietly poured half of the contents of the bottle into the wash bowl, where it speedily drained from sight!

"Don't catch me drinking such rot," he muttered to himself. "I'd rather have some good liquor any day," and he took a long pull from a black bottle he had in his valise.

About noon a carriage drove up to the hotel and two men alighted.

One led the way into the hotel and asked to see

the register.

"I'd like to see Mr. David Ball," said he to the clerk.

"Mr. Ball is sick."

"So I have heard and that is why I wish to see him."

"I'll send up your card."

"I don't happen to have a card. Tell him Mr. Anderson is here, from Philadelphia, with a friend of his."

The message was sent to the sick man's room, and word came down that he would see the visitors in a few minutes.

"He says he is pretty sick and he can't talk business very long," aid the bell boy.

"We won't bother him very much," answered the man who had given his name as Anderson.

Joe happened to be close by during this conversation and he looked the man called Anderson over with care.

"I've seen that man, too!" he declared to himself. "But where? I declare he is as much of a mystery as the sick one!"

Our hero's curiosity was now aroused to the highest pitch, and when the two men walked up to David Ball's room he followed to the very doorway.

"Come in," came from the room, and a deep groan followed. On the bed lay the man from Montana, wrapped in several blankets and with a look of anguish on his features.

"Feeling pretty bad, eh?" said Anderson, as he stalked in. "I am downright sorry for you."

"I'm afraid I am going to die," groaned the man in bed. "The doctor says I am in bad shape. He wants me to take a trip to Europe, or somewhere else."

"This is Mr. Maurice Vane," went on Anderson. "We won't trouble you any more than is necessary, Mr. Ball."

"I am sorry to disturb you," said Maurice Vane. He was a kindly looking gentleman. "Perhaps we had better defer this business until some other time."

"Oh, no, one time is as bad as another," came with another groan from the bed. "Besides, I admit I need money badly. If it wasn't for that - ". The man in bed began to cough. "Say, shut the door," he went on, to the first man who had come in.

The door was closed, and for the time being Joe heard no more of the conversation.

It must be admitted that our hero was perplexed, and with good reason. He felt certain that the man in bed was shamming, that he was hardly sick at all. If so, what was his game?

"Something is surely wrong somewhere," he reasoned. "I wish I could get to the bottom of it."

The room next to the one occupied by David Ball was

empty and he slipped into this. The room contained a closet, and on the other side was another closet, opening into the room the men were in. The partition between was of boards, and as the other door stood wide open, Joe, by placing his head to the boards, could hear fairly well.

"You have the stock?" he heard Maurice Vane ask.

"Yes, in my valise. Hand me the bag and I'll show you," answered the man in bed. "Oh, how weak I feel!" he sighed.

There was a silence and then the rustling of papers.

"And what is your bottom price for these?" went on Maurice Vane.

"Thirty thousand dollars."

"I told Mr. Vane you might possibly take twenty-five thousand," came from the man called Anderson.

"They ought to be worth face value - fifty thousand dollars," said the man in bed.

A talk in a lower tone followed, and then more rustling of papers.

"I will call to-morrow with the cash," said Maurice Vane, as he prepared to leave. "In the meantime, you promise to keep these shares for me?"

"I'll keep them until noon. I've got another offer," said the man in bed.

"We'll be back," put in the man called Anderson. "So don't you sell to anybody else."

Then the two visitors left and went downstairs. Five minutes later they were driving away in the direction of the railroad station.

"This certainly beats anything I ever met before," said Joe, to himself as he watched them go. "I'll wager all I am worth that I've met that Anderson before, and that he is a bad man. I do wish I could get at the bottom of what is going on."

In the evening he had occasion to go upstairs in the hotel once more. To his surprise he saw Mr. David Ball sitting in a rocking-chair, calmly smoking a cigar and reading a paper.

"He isn't as sick as he was this morning," he mused. "In fact, I don't think he is sick at all."

He wished to be on hand the following morning, when the strangers came back, but an errand took him up the lake. He had to stop at several places, and did not start on the return until four in the afternoon.

On his way back Joe went ashore close to where the old lodge was located, and something, he could not tell what, made him run over and take a look at the spot that had proved a shelter for Ned and himself during the heavy storm. How many things had occurred since that fatal day!

As our hero looked into one of the rooms he remembered the strange men he had seen there - the fellows who had talked about mining stocks. Then, of a sudden, a revelation came to him, like a thunderbolt out of a clear sky.

"I've got it! I've got it!" he cried. "Mr. David Ball is that fellow who called himself Malone, and Anderson is the man named Caven! They are both imposters!"

CHAPTER XI.

A FRUITLESS CHASE.

The more Joe thought over the matter the more he became convinced that he was right. He remembered a good deal of the talk he had overheard during the storm, although such talk had, for the time being, been driven from his mind by the tragic death of old Hiram Bodley.

"If they are working some game what can this Maurice Vane have to do with it?" he asked himself.

He thought it best to get back to the hotel at once, and tell Mr. Mallison of his suspicions. But, as luck would have it, scarcely had he started to row his boat again when an oarlock broke, and so it took him the best part of an hour to make the trip.

"Where is Mr. Mallison?" he asked of the clerk of the hotel.

"Out in the stable, I believe," was the answer.

Without waiting, our hero ran down to the stable and found the hotel proprietor inspecting some hay that had just been unloaded.

"I'd like to speak to you a moment, Mr. Mallison," he said. "It's important," and he motioned for the man to follow him.

"What is it, Joe?"

"It's about those men who called to see that sick man, and about the sick man, too."

"He has gone - all of them have gone."

"What!" ejaculated our hero. "The sick man, too?"

"Exactly. But he didn't go with the others. While they were here he was in bed, but right after they left he arose, dressed himself, and drove away."

"Where did he go to?"

"I don't know."

"Do you know what became of the other two men?"

"I do not. But what's up? Is there anything wrong?" questioned the hotel proprietor, with a look of concern on his face.

"I am afraid there is," answered Joe, and told his tale from beginning to end.

"That's an odd sort of a yarn, Joe. It's queer you didn't recognize the men before.

"It is queer, sir, but I can't help that. It flashed over me just as I looked into the window of the old lodge."

"You haven't made any mistake?"

"No, sir."

"Humph!" Andrew Mallison mused for a moment. "I don't really see what I can do in the matter. We can't prove that those men are wrongdoers, can we?"

"Not unless they tried some game on this Mr. Maurice Vane."

"They may have sold him some worthless mining shares. That sort of a trick is rather old."

"I think we ought to make a search for this David Ball, or Malone, or whatever his name is."

"I'm willing to do that."

After questioning half a dozen people they learned that the pretended sick man had driven off in the direction of a village called Hopedale.

"What made him go there, do you think?" questioned Joe.

"I don't know, excepting that he thought of getting a train on the other line."

A horse and buggy were procured, and in this Mr. Mallison and our hero drove over to Hopedale. They were still on the outskirts of the village when they heard a locomotive whistle.

"There's the afternoon train now!" cried Joe. "Perhaps it's the one he wants to catch."

The horse was touched up and the buggy drove up to the railroad platform at breakneck speed. But the train was gone and all they could see of it was the last car as it swung around one of the mountain bends.

"Too late, Mr. Mallison!" sang out the station master. "If I had known ye was comin' I might have held her up a bit."

"I didn't want the train, Jackson. Who got on board?"

"Two ladies, a man and a boy - Dick Fadder."

"Did you know the man?"

"No."

"What did he have with him?"

"A dress suit case."

"Was he dressed in a dark blue suit and wear a slouch hat?" asked Joe.

"Yes, and had a light overcoat with him."

"That was our man."

"Anything wrong with him?" asked the station master.

"Perhaps," answered the hotel proprietor. "Anyway, we wanted to see him. Did he buy a ticket?"

"Yes, to Snagtown."

"What can he want in Snagtown?" asked Joe.

"Oh, that might have been a blind, Joe. He could easily go through to Philadelphia or some other place, if he wanted to."

At first they thought of telegraphing ahead to stop the man, but soon gave that plan up. They had no evidence, and did not wish to make trouble unless they knew exactly what they were doing.

"I hope it turns out all right," observed Andrew Mallison, when they were driving back to Riverside. "If there was a swindle it would give my hotel a black eye."

"That's one reason why I wanted that man held," answered Joe.

The next day and that following passed quietly, and our hero began to think that he had made a mistake and misjudged the men. He was kept very busy and so almost forgot the incident.

Among the new boarders was a fussy old man named Chaster, who was speedily nicknamed by the bell boys Chestnuts. He was a particular individual, and made everybody as uncomfortable as he possibly could.

One day Wilberforce Chaster - to use his full name, - asked Joe to take him out on the lake for a day's fishing. Our hero readily complied, and was in hot water from the time they went out until they returned. Nothing suited the old man, and as he caught hardly any fish he was exceedingly put out when he came back to the hotel.

"Your boatman is of no account," he said to Andrew

Mallison. "I have spent a miserable day," and he stamped off to his room in high anger.

"It was not my fault, Mr. Mallison," said Joe, with burning cheeks. "I did my level best by him."

"That man has been making trouble for us ever since he come," answered the hotel proprietor. "I am going to ask him to go elsewhere when his week is up."

The insults that Joe had received that day from Wilberforce Chaster rankled in his mind, and he determined to square accounts with the boarder if he possibly could.

Towards evening he met a bell boy named Harry Ross who had also had trouble with Chaster, and the two talked the matter over.

"We ought to get square," said Harry Ross. "I wish I could souse him with a pitcher of ice water."

"I've got a plan," said Joe.

Stopping at the hotel was a traveling doctor, who came to Riverside twice a year, for a stay of two weeks each time. He sold some patent medicines, and had in his room several skulls and also a skeleton strung on wires.

"That doctor is away," said our hero. "I wonder if we can't smuggle the skulls and the skeleton into Mr. Chaster's room?"

"Just the cheese!" cried the bell boy, enthusiastically. "And let us rub the bones with some of those matches that glow in the dark!"

The plan was talked over, and watching their chance the two transferred the skeleton and the skulls to the apartment occupied by Wilberforce Chaster. Then they rubbed phosphorus on the bones, and hung them upon long strings, running over a doorway into the next room.

That evening Wilberforce Chaster remained in the hotel parlor until ten o 'clock. Then he marched off to his room in his usual ill humor. The gas was lit and he went to bed without delay.

As soon as the light went out and they heard the man retire, Joe and the bell boy began to groan in an ominous manner. As they did so, they worked the strings to which the skulls and the skeleton were attached, causing them to dance up and down in the center of the old man's room.

Hearing the groans, Wilberforce Chaster sat up in bed and listened. Then he peered around in the darkness.

"Ha! what is that?" he gasped, as he caught sight of the skulls. "Am I dreaming - or is that - Oh!"

He started and began to shake from head to foot, for directly in front of him was the skeleton, moving up and down in a jerky fashion and glowing with a dull fire. His hair seemed to stand on end. He dove under the coverings of the bed.

"The room is haunted!" he moaned. "Was ever such a thing seen before! This is wretched! Whatever shall I do?"

The groans continued, and presently he gave another look from under the bed clothes. The skeleton appeared to be coming nearer. He gave a loud yell of anguish.

"Go away! Go away! Oh, I am haunted by a ghost! This is awful! I cannot stand it!"

He fairly tumbled out of bed and caught up his clothing in a heap. Then, wrapped in some comfortables, he burst out of the room and ran down the hallway like a person possessed of the evil spirits.

"Come be quick, or we'll get caught!" whispered Joe, and ran into the room, followed by the bell boy. In a trice they pulled loose the strings that held the skulls and the skeleton, and restored the things to the doctor's room from which they had been taken. Then they went below by a back stairs.

The whole hotel was in an alarm, and soon Mr. Mallison came upon the scene.

"What is the meaning of this?" he demanded, severely, of Wilberforce Chaster.

"The meaning is, sir, that your hotel is haunted," was the answer, which startled all who heard it.

Horatio Alger Jr.

CHAPTER XII.

THE PARTICULARS OF A SWINDLE.

"This hotel haunted?" gasped the proprietor. "Sir, you are mistaken. Such a thing is impossible."

"It is true," insisted Mr. Wilberforce Chaster. "I shall not stay here another night."

"What makes you think it is haunted?"

"There is a ghost in my room."

"Oh!" shrieked a maid who had come on the scene. "A ghost! I shall not stay either!"

"What kind of a ghost?" demanded Andrew Mallison.

"A - er - a skeleton - and some skulls! I saw them with my own eyes," went on the victim. "Come and see them for yourself."

"This is nonsense," said the hotel proprietor. "I will go and convince you that you are mistaken."

He led the way and half a dozen followed, including Wilberforce Chaster, who kept well to the rear. Just as the party reached the door of the apartment Joe and the bell boy came up.

Without hesitation Andrew Mallison threw open the door of the room and looked inside. Of course he saw nothing out of the ordinary.

"Where is your ghost?" he demanded. "I see nothing of it."

"Don't - don't you see - er - a skeleton?" demanded the man who had been victimized.

"I do not."

Trembling in every limb Wilberforce Chaster came forward and peered into the room.

"Well?" demanded the hotel proprietor, after a pause.

"I - I certainly saw them."

"Then where are they now?"

"I - I don't know."

By this time others were crowding into the apartment. All gazed around, and into the clothes closet, but found nothing unusual.

"You must be the victim of some hallucination, sir," said the hotel proprietor, severely.

He hated to have anything occur which might give his establishment a bad reputation.

"No, sir, I saw the things with my own eyes."

The matter was talked over for several minutes longer and then the hired help was ordered away.

"I shall not stay in this room," insisted Wilberforce Chaster.

"You need not remain in the hotel," answered Andrew Mallison, quickly. "You can leave at once. You have alarmed the whole establishment needlessly."

Some warm words followed, and the upshot of the matter was that the fussy old boarder had to pack his things and seek another hotel that very night.

"I am glad to get rid of him," said the hotel proprietor, after Wilberforce Chaster had departed. "He was making trouble all the time."

"We fixed him, didn't we?" said the bell boy to Joe.

"I hope it teaches him a lesson to be more considerate in the future," answered our hero.

Several days passed and Joe had quite a few parties to take out on the lake. The season was now drawing to a close, and our hero began to wonder what he had best do when boating was over.

"I wonder if I couldn't strike something pretty good in Philadelphia?" he asked himself. The idea of going to one of the big cities appealed to him strongly.

One afternoon, on coming in from a trip across the lake, Joe found Andrew Mallison in conversation with Mr. Maurice Vane, who had arrived at the hotel scarcely an hour before. The city man was evidently both excited and disappointed.

"Here is the boy now," said the hotel proprietor, and called Joe up.

"Well, young man, I guess you have hit the truth," were Maurice Vane's first words.

"About those other fellows?" asked our hero, quickly.

"That's it."

"Did they swindle you?"

"They did."

"By selling you some worthless mining stocks?"

"Yes. If you will, I'd like you to tell me all you can about those two men."

"I will," answered Joe, and told of the strange meeting at the old lodge and of what had followed. Maurice Vane drew a long breath and shook his head sadly.

"I was certainly a green one, to be taken in so slyly," said he.

"How did they happen to hear of you?" questioned Joe, curiously.

"I answered an advertisement in the daily paper," said Maurice Vane. "Then this man, Caven, or whatever his right name may be, came to me and said he had a certain plan for making a good deal of money. All I had to do was to invest a certain amount and inside of a few days I could clear fifteen or twenty thousand dollars."

"That was surely a nice proposition," said Joe, with a smile.

"I agreed to go into the scheme if it was all plain sailing and then this Caven gave me some of the details. He said there was a demand for a certain kind of mining shares. He knew an old miner who was sick and who was willing to sell the shares he possessed for a reasonable sum of money. The plan was to buy the shares and then sell them to another party - a broker - at a big advance in price."

"That was simple enough," put in Andrew Mallison.

"Caven took me to see a man who called himself a broker. He had an elegant office and looked prosperous. He told us he would be glad to buy certain mining shares at a certain figure if he could get them in the near future. He said a client was red-hot after the shares. I questioned him closely and he appeared to be a truthful man. He said some folks wanted to buy out the mine and consolidate it with another mine close by."

"And then you came here and bought the stock of Malone?" queried Joe.

"Yes. Caven made me promise to give him half the profits and I agreed. I came here, and as you know, Malone, or Ball, or whatever his name is, pretended to be very sick and in need of money. He set his price, and I came back with the cash and took the mining stock. I was to meet Caven, alias Anderson, the next day and go to the broker with him, but Caven did not appear. Then I grew suspicious and went to see the broker alone. The man was gone and the office locked up. After that I asked some other brokers about the stock, and they told me it was not worth five cents on the dollar."

"Isn't there any such mine at all?" asked Joe.

"Oh, yes, there is such a mine, but it was abandoned two years ago, after ten thousand dollars had been sunk in it. They said it paid so little that it was not worth considering."

"That is certainly too bad for you," said Joe. "And you can't find any trace of Caven or Malone?"

"No, both of the rascals have disappeared completely. I tried to trace Caven and his broker friend in Philadelphia but it was of no use. More than likely they have gone to some place thousands of miles away."

"Yes, and probably this Ball, or Malone, has joined them," put in Andrew Mallison. "Mr. Vane, I am exceedingly sorry for you."

"I am sorry for myself, but I deserve my loss, for being such a fool," went on the victim.

"Have you notified the police?" asked Joe.

"Oh, yes, and I have hired a private detective to do what he can, too. But I am afraid my money is gone for good."

"You might go and reopen the mine, Mr. Vane."

"Thank you, but I have lost enough already, without throwing good money after bad, as the saying is."

"It may be that that detective will find the swindlers, sooner or later."

"Such a thing is, of course, possible, but I am not over sanguine."

"I am afraid your money is gone for good," broke in Andrew Mallison. "I wish I could help you, but I don't see how I can."

The matter was talked over for a good hour, and all three visited the room Malone had occupied, which had been vacant ever since. But a hunt around revealed nothing of value, and they returned to the office.

"I can do nothing more for you, Mr. Vane," said Andrew Mallison.

"I wish I could do something," said Joe. Something about Maurice Vane was very attractive to him.

"If you ever hear of these rascals let me know," continued the hotel proprietor.

"I will do so," was the reply.

With that the conversation on the subject closed. Maurice Vane remained at the hotel overnight and left by the early train on the following morning.

CHAPTER XIII.

OFF FOR THE CITY.

"Joe, our season ends next Saturday."

"I know it, Mr. Mallison."

"We are going to close the house on Tuesday. It won't pay to keep open after our summer boarders leave."

"I know that, too."

"Have you any idea what you intend to do?" went on the hotel proprietor. He was standing down by the dock watching Joe clean out one of the boats.

"I'm thinking of going to Philadelphia."

"On a visit?"

"No, sir, to try my luck."

"Oh, I see. It's a big city, my lad."

"I know it, but, somehow, I feel I might do better there than in such a town as this, - and I am getting tired of hanging around the lake."

"There is more money in Philadelphia than there is here, that is certain, Joe. But you can't always get hold of it. The big cities are crowded with people trying to obtain situations."

"I'm sure I can find something to do, Mr. Mallison. And, by the way, when I leave, will you give me a written recommendation?"

"Certainly. You have done well since you came here. But you had better think twice before going to Philadelphia."

"I've thought it over more than twice. I don't expect the earth, but I feel that I can get something to do before my money runs out."

"How much money have you saved up?"

"I've got fifty-six dollars, and I'm going to sell my boat for four dollars."

"Well, sixty dollars isn't such a bad capital. I have known men to start out with a good deal less. When I left home I had but twenty dollars and an extra suit of clothes."

"Did you come from a country place?"

"No, I came from New York. Times were hard and I couldn't get a single thing to do. I went to Paterson, New Jersey, and got work in a silk mill. From there I went to Camden, and then to Philadelphia. From Philadelphia I came here and have been here ever since."

"You have been prosperous."

"Fairly so, although I don't make as much money as some of the hotel men in the big cities. But then they take larger risks. A few years ago a hotel friend of mine opened a big hotel in Atlantic City. He hoped to make a small fortune, but he was not located in the right part of the town and at the end of the season he found himself just fifteen thousand dollars out of pocket. Now he has sold out and is running a country hotel fifty miles west of here. He doesn't hope to make so much, but his business is much safer."

"I'm afraid it will be a long time before I get money enough to run a hotel," laughed our hero.

"Would you like to run one?"

"I don't know. I'd like to educate myself first."

"Don't you study some now? I have seen you with some arithmetics and histories."

"Yes, sir, I study a little every day. You see, I never had much schooling, and I don't want to grow up ignorant, if I can help it."

"That is the proper spirit, lad," answered Andrew Mallison, warmly. "Learn all you possibly can. It will always be the means of doing you good."

The conversation took place on Thursday and two days later the season at the summer hotel came to an end and the last of the boarders took their departure. Monday was spent in putting things in order, and by Tuesday afternoon work around the place came to an end, and all the help was paid off.

In the meantime Joe had sold his boat. With all of his money in his pocket he called at the Talmadge house to see if Ned had returned from the trip to the west.

"Just got back yesterday," said Ned, who came to greet him. "Had a glorious trip. I wish you had been along. I like traveling better than staying at home all the time."

"I am going to do a bit of traveling myself, Ned."

"Where are you going?"

"To Philadelphia - to try my luck in that city."

"Going to leave Mr. Mallison?"

"Yes, - the season is at an end."

"Oh, I see. So you are going to the Quaker City, as pa calls it. I wish you luck. You'll have to write to me, Joe, and let me know how you are getting along."

"I will, - and you must write to me."

"Of course."

On the following day Joe rowed along the lake to where his old home dock had been located and made a trip to what was left of the cabin. He spent another hour in hunting for the blue box, but without success.

"I suppose I'll never find that box," he sighed. "I may as well give up thinking about it."

From Andrew Mallison our hero had obtained his letter of recommendation and also a good pocket map of Philadelphia. The hotel man had also made him a present of a neat suit case, in which he packed his few belongings.

Ned Talmadge came to see him off at the depot. The day was cool and clear, and Joe felt in excellent spirits.

Soon the train came along and our hero got aboard, along with a dozen or fifteen others. He waved a hand to Ned and his friend shouted out a good-bye. Then the train moved on, and the town was soon left in the distance.

The car that Joe had entered was not more than quarter filled and he easily found a seat for himself by a window. He placed his suit case at his feet and then gave himself up to looking at the scenery as it rushed past.

Joe had never spent much of his time on the railroad, so the long ride had much of novelty in it. The scenery was grand, as they wound in and out among the hills and mountains, or crossed brooks and rivers and well-kept farms. Numerous stops were made, and long before Philadelphia was gained the train became crowded.

"Nice day for riding," said a man who sat down beside our hero. He looked to be what he was, a prosperous farmer.

"It is," answered Joe.

"Goin' to Philadelphy, I reckon," went on the farmer.

"Yes, sir."

"That's where I'm going, too. Got a little business to attend to."

"I am going there to try my luck," said Joe, he felt he could talk to the old man with confidence.

"Goin' to look fer a job, eh?"

"Yes, sir."

"Wot kin ye do, if I might ask?"

"Oh, I'm willing to do most anything. I've been taking care of rowboats and working around a summer hotel, at Lake Tandy."

"Well, ye won't git many boats to look at down to Philadelphy!" and the old farmer chuckled.

"I suppose not. Maybe I'll strike a job at one of the hotels."

"Perhaps. They tell me some hotels down there is monsterous - ten an' twelve stories high. Ye don't catch me goin' to no sech place. In case o' fire, it's all up with ye, if you're on the twelfth story."

"Are you going to Philadelphia to stay, Mr.-"

"Bean is my name - Josiah Bean. I'm from Haydown Center, I am. Got a farm there o' a hundred acres."

"Oh, is that so!"

"Wot's your handle, young man?"

"My name is Joe Bodley. I came from Riverside."

"Proud to know you." And Josiah Bean shook hands. "No, I ain't going to stay in Philadelphy. I'm a-going on business fer my wife. A relative left her some property an' I'm a-goin' to collect on it."

"That's a pleasant trip to be on," was our hero's comment.

"I'll feel better when I have the six hundred dollars in my fist. I'm afraid it ain't goin' to be no easy matter to git it."

"What's the trouble!"

"I ain't known in Philadelphy an' they tell me a feller has got to be identified or somethin' like thet - somebody has got to speak for ye wot knows ye."

"I see. Perhaps you'll meet some friend."

"Thet's wot I'm hopin' fer."

The train rolled on and presently Joe got out his map and began to study it, so that he might know something of the great city when he arrived there.

"Guess I'll git a drink o' water," said Josiah Bean, and walked to the end of the car to do so. Immediately a slick looking man who had been seated behind the farmer arose and followed him.

CHAPTER XIV.

A SCENE ON THE TRAIN.

The slick-looking individual had listened attentively to all that passed between our hero and the farmer.

He waited until the latter had procured his drink of water and then rushed up with a smile on his face.

"I declare!" he exclaimed. "How do you do?" And he extended his hand.

"How do you do?" repeated the farmer, shaking hands slowly. He felt much perplexed, for he could not remember having met the other man before.

"How are matters up on the farm?" went on the stranger.

"Thank you, very good."

"I - er - I don't think you remember me, Mr. Bean," went on the slick-looking individual.

"Well, somehow I think I know your face," answered the old farmer, lamely. He did not wish to appear wanting in politeness.

"You ought to remember me. I spent some time in Haydown Center year before last, selling machines."

"Oh, you had them patent reapers, is that it?"

"You've struck it."

"I remember you now. You're a nephew of Judge Davis."

"Exactly."

"O' course! O' course! But I can't remember your name nohow."

"It's Davis, too - Henry Davis."

"Oh, yes. I'm glad to meet you, Mr. Davis."

"I saw you in the seat with that boy," went on the man we shall call Henry Davis. "I thought I knew you from the start, but I wasn't dead sure. Going to Philadelphia with us?"

"Yes, sir."

"Good enough. Mr. Bean, won't you smoke with me? I was just going into the smoker."

"Thanks, but I - er - I don't smoke much."

"Just one mild cigar. That won't hurt you, I'm sure. I love to meet old friends," continued Henry Davis.

In the end the old farmer was pursuaded to walk into the smoking car and here the slick-looking individual found a corner seat where they would be undisturbed.

"I expect to spend a week or more in Philadelphia, Mr. Bean," said the stranger; "if I can be of service to you during that time, command me."

"Well, perhaps ye can be of service to me. Do ye know many folks in the city?"

"Oh, yes, a great many. Some are business friends and some are folks in high society."

"I don't care for no high society. But I've got to collect six hundred dollars an' I want somebody to identify me."

"Oh, I can do that easily, Mr. Bean."

"Kin ye?" The farmer grew interested at once. "If ye kin I'll be much obliged to ye."

"Where must you be identified?"

"Down to the office of Barwell & Cameron, on Broad street. Do ye know 'em?"

"I know of them, and I can find somebody who does know them, so there will not be the least trouble."

"It's a load off my mind," said Josiah Bean, with a sigh. "Ye see, the money is comin' to my wife. She writ to 'em that I was comin' to collect an' they writ back it would be all right, only I would have to be identified. Jest as if everybody in Haydown Center don't know I'm Josiah Bean an' a piller in the Union Church down there, an' a cousin to Jedge Bean o' Lassindale."

"Well, they have to be mighty particular when they pay out any money in the city. There are so many sharpers around."

"I ain't no sharper."

"To be sure you are not, and neither am I. But I once had trouble getting money."

"Is thet so?"

"Yes. But after I proved who I was the folks were pretty well ashamed of themselves," went on Henry Davis, smoothly.

So the talk ran on and at the end of half an hour the old farmer and the slick-looking individual were on exceedingly friendly terms. Henry Davis asked much about the old man and gathered in a good stock of information.

When Philadelphia was gained it was dark, and coming out of the big railroad station Joe at first knew not which way to turn. The noise and the crowd of people confused him.

"Have a cab? Carriage?" bawled the hackmen.

"Paper!" yelled a newsboy. "All the evenin' papers!"

"Smash yer baggage!" called out a luggage boy, not near as tall as our hero.

Looking ahead, Joe saw Josiah Bean and the

slick-looking individual moving down the street and without realizing it, our hero began to follow the pair.

"He must be some friend," said our hero to himself.

He wondered where they were going and his curiosity getting the better of him he continued to follow them for half a dozen blocks. At last they came to a halt in front of a building displaying the sign:

JOHNSON'S QUAKER HOTEL

MODERATE TERMS FOR ALL.

"This hotel is all right and the prices are right, too," Joe heard the slick-looking man tell the old farmer.

"Then thet suits me," answered Josiah Bean. "I'll go in an' git a room fer the night."

"I think I might as well do the same," said Henry Davis. "I don't care to go away over to my boarding house at Fairmount Park."

The pair walked into the hotel, and Joe saw them register and pass down the corridor in the company of a bell boy. Then our hero entered the place.

"Can I get a room here for the night?" he asked of the clerk behind the desk.

"Certainly."

"What is the charge?"

"Seventy-five cents."

"That suits me."

The register was shoved forward and Joe wrote down his name. Then he was shown to a small room on the third floor. The building was but four stories high.

Joe was tired and soon went to bed. In the next room he heard a murmur of voices and made out that the old farmer and his friend were talking earnestly.

"They must be very friendly," was his comment, and thinking the matter over he fell asleep.

Bright and early in the morning our hero arose, dressed himself, and went below. He had breakfast in the restaurant attached to the hotel and was just finishing up when the old farmer and the slick-looking individual came in.

"Hullo!" cried Josiah Bean. "What are you doin' here?"

"I got a room overnight," answered our hero.

"We're stopping here, too. This is my friend, Mr. Henry Davis."

"Good morning," said the slick-looking man. He did not seem to fancy meeting Joe.

They sat down close at hand and, while eating, the farmer asked Joe half a dozen questions.

He spoke about his own business until Henry Davis nudged him in the side.

"I wouldn't tell that boy too much," he said in a

Horatio Alger Jr.

low tone.

"Oh, he's all right," answered the old farmer.

Joe heard the slick-looking individual's words and they made his face burn. He looked at the man narrowly and made up his mind he was not a fellow to be desired for an acquaintance.

Having finished, our hero paid his bill and left the restaurant. He scarcely knew which way to turn, but resolved to look over the newspapers first and see if any positions were offered.

While in the reading room he saw Josiah Bean and his acquaintance leave the hotel and walk in the direction of Broad street.

A little later Joe took from the paper he was reading the addresses of several people who wanted help, and then he, too, left the hotel.

The first place he called at was a florist's establishment, but the pay was so small he declined the position.

"I could not live on three dollars per week," he said.

"That is all we care to pay," answered the proprietor, coldly. "It is more than other establishments pay."

"Then I pity those who work at the other places," returned Joe, and walked out.

CHAPTER XV.

WHAT HAPPENED TO JOSIAH BEAN.

In the meantime Josiah Bean and the slick-looking individual turned into Broad street and made their way to a certain establishment known as the Eagle's Club.

Here Henry Davis called another man aside.

"Say, Foxy, do you know anybody down to Barwell & Cameron's?" he asked, in a low tone, so that the old farmer could not hear.

"Yes - a clerk named Chase."

"Then come down and introduce me."

"What's the game?"

"Never mind - there's a tenner in it for you if it works."

"Then I'm on, Bill."

"Hush - my name is Henry Davis."

"All right, Hank," returned Foxy, carelessly.

He came forward and was introduced to the old farmer

in the following fashion:

"Mr. Richard Barlow - of Barlow & Small, manufacturers."

All three made their way to the establishment of Barwell & Cameron, and then Henry Davis was introduced under that name to a clerk.

As soon as Foxy had departed the slick-looking individual turned to the clerk and called the old farmer forward.

"This is my esteemed friend, Mr. Josiah Bean, of Haydown Center. He has business with Mr. Cameron, I believe."

"I'm here to collect six hundred dollars," said Josiah Bean. "Mr. Cameron writ me some letters about it."

"Very well, sir. Sit down, gentlemen, and I'll tell Mr. Cameron."

The two were kept waiting for a few minutes and were then ushered into a private office. Through Chase, the clerk, Henry Davis was introduced and then Josiah Bean. All the papers proved to be correct, and after the old farmer had signed his name he was given a check.

"See here, I want the cash," he demanded.

"Very well," said Mr. Cameron. "Indorse the check and I'll have the money drawn for you across the street."

The farmer wrote down his name once more, and a few minutes later received his six hundred dollars in twelve brand-new fifty-dollar bills.

"Gosh! Them will be nice fer Mirandy to look at," was his comment, as he surveyed the bills.

"Be careful that you don't lose them, Mr. Bean," cautioned Henry Davis, as the two left the establishment.

"Reckon the best thing I can do is to git back to hum this afternoon," remarked Josiah Bean, when he was on the street.

"Oh, now you are in town you'll have to look around a bit," said the slick-looking individual. "You can take a train back to-morrow just as well. Let me show you a few of the sights."

This tickled the old farmer and he agreed to remain over until the next noon. Then Henry Davis dragged the old man around to various points of interest and grew more familiar than ever.

While they were at the top of one of the big office buildings Henry Davis pretended to drop his pocketbook.

"How careless of me!" he cried.

"Got much in it?" queried Josiah Bean.

"Three thousand dollars."

"Do tell! It's a powerful sight o' money to carry so careless like."

"It is. Maybe you had better carry it for me, Mr. Bean."

"Not me! I ain't goin' to be responsible fer nobody's money but my own - an' Mirandy's."

"Better see if your own money is safe."

Josiah Bean got out his wallet and counted the bills.

"Safe enough."

"Are you sure? I thought there was only five hundred and fifty."

"No, six hundred."

"I'll bet you ten dollars on it."

"What! can't I count straight," gasped the old farmer, much disturbed. "Six hundred I tell you," he added, after he had gone over the amount once more.

"If there is I'll give you the ten dollars," answered the slick one. "Let me count the bills."

"All right, there ye be, Mr. Davis."

Henry Davis took the wallet and pretended to count the bills.

"Hullo, what's that?" he cried, whirling around.

"What's wot?" demanded Josiah Bean, also looking around.

"I thought I heard somebody cry fire."

"Don't say thet! Say, let's git out o' here - I don't want to look at the sights."

"All right - here's your money. I guess it's six hundred after all," answered the slick- looking individual, passing over the wallet.

They hurried to the elevator and got into quite a crowd of people.

"Wait for me here," said Henry Davis, as they walked past the side corridor. "I want to step in yonder office and send a message to a friend."

He ran off, leaving the old farmer by himself. Josiah Bean looked around him nervously.

"I guess that wasn't no cry o' fire after all," he mused. "Well, if there's a fire I kin git out from here quick enough."

The office building was a large one, running from one street to the next. On the street in the rear was a bookstore, the proprietor of which had advertised for a clerk.

Joe had applied for the position and was waiting for the proprietor to address him when, on chancing to look up, he saw Henry Davis rush past as if in a tremendous hurry.

"Hullo, that's the fellow who was with the old farmer," he told himself.

"What can I do for you, young man?" asked the proprietor of the bookshop, approaching at that instant.

"I believe you wish a clerk," answered our hero.

"Have you had experience in this line?"

"No, sir."

"Then you won't do. I must have someone who is experienced."

"I am willing to learn."

"It won't do. I want an experienced clerk or none at all," was the sharp answer.

Leaving the bookstore, Joe stood out on the sidewalk for a moment and then walked around the corner.

A moment later he caught sight of Josiah Bean, gazing up and down the thoroughfare and acting like one demented.

"What's the matter?" he asked.

"Matter?" bawled the old farmer. I've been took in! Robbed! Swindled! Oh, wot will Mirandy say!"

"Who robbed you?"

"Thet Mr. Davis I reckon! He counted the money last, an' now it's gone!"

"I saw Mr. Davis a minute ago."

"Where?"

"Around the corner, walking as fast as he could."

"He's got my money! Oh, I must catch him!"

"I'll help you," answered Joe, with vigor. "I thought he looked like a slick one," he added.

He led the way and Josiah Bean came behind. The old farmer looked as if he was ready to drop with fright. The thought of losing his wife's money was truly horrifying.

"Mirandy won't never forgive me!" he groaned. "Oh, say, boy, we've got to catch that rascal!"

"If we can," added our hero.

He had noted the direction taken by the swindler, and now ran across the street and into a side thoroughfare leading to where a new building was being put up.

Here, from a workman, he learned that the sharper had boarded a street car going south. He hailed the next car and both he and the old farmer got aboard.

"This ain't much use," said Josiah Bean, with quivering lips. "We dunno how far he took himself to."

"Let us trust to luck to meet him," said Joe.

They rode for a distance of a dozen blocks and then the car came to a halt, for there was a blockade ahead.

"We may as well get off," said our hero. "He may be in one of the forward cars."

They alighted and walked on, past half a dozen cars. Then our hero gave a cry of triumph .

"There he is!" he said, and pointed to the swindler, who stood on a car platform, gazing anxiously ahead.

CHAPTER XVI.

A MATTER OF SIX HUNDRED DOLLARS.

"Say, you, give me my money!"

Such were Josiah Bean's words, as he rushed up to Henry Davis and grabbed the swindler by the shoulder.

The slick-looking individual was thoroughly startled, for he had not dreamed that the countryman would get on his track so soon. He turned and looked at the man and also at Joe, and his face fell.

"Wha - what are you talking about?" he stammered.

"You know well enough what I am talking about," answered Josiah Bean, wrathfully. "I want my money, every cent o' it, - an' you are a-goin' to jail!"

"Sir, you are making a sad mistake," said the swindler, slowly. "I know nothing of you or your money."

"Yes, you do."

"Make him get off the car," put in Joe.

"Boy, what have you to do with this?" asked the swindler, turning bitterly to our hero.

"Not much perhaps," answered Joe. "But I'd like to see justice done."

"I want that money," went on the countryman, doggedly. "Come off the car."

He caught the swindler tighter than ever and made him walk to the sidewalk. By this time a crowd of people began to collect.

"What's the trouble here?" asked one gentleman.

"He's robbed me, that's what's the matter," answered the countryman. "He has got six hundred dollars o' mine!"

"Six hundred dollars!" cried several and began to take a deeper interest.

"Gentleman this man must be crazy. I never saw him before," came loudly from the swindler.

"That is not true!" cried Joe. "He was with the man who lost the money. I saw them together yesterday."

"I am a respectable merchant from Pittsburg," went on the swindler. "It is outrageous to be accused in this fashion."

"Somebody had better call a policeman," said Joe.

"I'll do dat," answered a newsboy, and ran off to execute the errand.

As the crowd began to collect the swindler saw that he was going to have difficulty in clearing himself or getting away. He looked around, and seeing an opening made a dash for it.

He might have gotten away had it not been for Joe. But our hero was watching him with the eyes of a hawk, and quick as a flash he caught the rascal by the coat sleeve.

"No, you don't!" he exclaimed. "Come back here!"

"Let go!" cried the man and hit Joe in the ear. But the blow did not stop Joe from detaining him and in a second more Josiah Bean caught hold also.

"Ain't goin' to git away nohow!" exclaimed the countryman, and took hold of the swindler's throat.

"Le - let go!" came back in a gasp. "Don't - don't strangle me!"

When a policeman arrived the swindler was thoroughly cowed and he turned reproachfully to Josiah Bean.

"This isn't fair," he said. It was all a joke. I haven't got your money."

"Yes, you have."

"He is right, Mr. Bean," put in Joe. "The money, I think, is in your side pocket."

The countryman searched the pocket quickly and brought out a flat pocketbook.

"Hullo! this ain't mine!" he ejaculated.

He opened the pocketbook and inside were the twelve fifty-dollar bills.

"My money sure enough! How in the world did it git there?"

"This man just slipped the pocketbook into your pocket," answered Joe.

"I did not!" put in the swindler, hotly.

"You did."

"Dat's right!" piped up the newsboy who had brought the policeman. "I see him do de trick jest a minit ago!"

"This is a plot against me!" fumed the swindler.

"Dat feller is a bad egg!" went on the news- boy. "His name is Bill Butts. He's a slick one, he is. Hits de country jays strong, he does!"

At the mention of the name, Bill Butts, the policeman became more interested than ever.

"You'll come to the station house with me," he said, sternly. "We can straighten out the matter there."

"All right," answered Bill Butts, for such was his real name.

In a few minutes more the party, including Joe, was off in the direction of the police station.

"Better keep a good eye on your money, Mr. Bean," said our hero, as they walked along.

"I've got it tucked away safe in an inside pocket," answered the old countryman.

The station house was several squares away, and while walking beside the policeman the eyes of Bill Butts were wide open, looking for some means of escape. He had "done time" twice and he did not wish to be sent up again if it could possibly be avoided.

His opportunity came in an unexpected manner. In a show window on a corner a man was exhibiting some new athletic appliances and a crowd had collected to witness the exhibition. The policeman had to force his way through.

"Hi, quit shovin' me!" growled a burly fellow in the crowd, not knowing he was addressing a guardian of the law.

"Make way here!" ordered the policeman, sternly, and then the fellow fell back.

It gave Bill Butts the chance he wanted and as quick as a flash he dove into the crowd and out of sight.

"He is running away!" cried Joe.

"Catch him!" put in Josiah Bean.

Both went after the swindler and so did the policeman. But the crowd was too dense for them, and inside of five minutes Bill Butts had made good his escape.

"What did ye want to let him slip ye fer?" growled the old countryman, angrily.

"Don't talk to me," growled the policeman.

"He ought to be reported for this," put in our hero.

"Say another word and I'll run you both in," said the bluecoat.

"Come away," whispered Josiah Bean. "Anyway, it ain't so bad. I've got my money."

"I'm willing to go," answered Joe. "But, just the same, that policeman is a pudding head," he added, loudly.

"I'll pudding head you!" cried the bluecoat, but made no attempt to molest Joe, whose general style he did not fancy.

Side by side Josiah Bean and our hero walked away, until the crowd was left behind and they were practically alone.

"I'm goin' to count thet money again," said the old countryman, and did so, to make certain that it was all there.

"We were lucky to spot the rascal, Mr. Bean."

"I didn't spot him - it was you. I'm much obliged to ye."

"Oh, that's all right."

"Seems to me you are entitled to a reward, Joe," went on the old farmer.

"I don't want any reward."

"But you're a-goin' to take it. How would five dollars strike you?"

"Not at all, sir. I don't want a cent."

"Then, maybe, ye won't even come an' take dinner with me," continued the old man, in disappointed tones.

"Yes, I'll do that, for this chase has made me tremendously hungry."

"If ye ever come down my way, Joe, ye must stop an' call on me."

"I will, Mr. Bean."

"Nuthin' on my farm will be too good for ye, Joe. I'm goin' to tell my wife Mirandy o' this happenin' an' she'll thank you jest as I've done."

A good restaurant was found not far away and there the two procured a fine meal and took their time eating it.

"Have ye found work yet?" asked the old man.

"Not yet. I was looking for a job when I met you."

"Well, I hope ye strike wot ye want, lad. But it's hard to git a place in the city, some times."

"I shall try my level best."

"Wish I could git a job fer ye. But I don't know nubuddy."

"I am going to try the hotels next. I have a strong letter of recommendation from a hotel man."

"If ye don't git no work in Philadelphy come out on my farm. I'll board ye all winter fer nuthin'," went on Josiah Bean, generously.

"Thank you, Mr. Bean; you are very kind."

"I mean it. We don't live very high-falutin', but we have plenty o' plain, good victuals."

"I'll remember what you say," answered our hero.

An hour later he saw the countryman on a train bound for home, and then he started once more to look for a situation.

CHAPTER XVII.

JOE'S NEW POSITION.

All of that afternoon Joe looked for a position among the various hotels of the Quaker City. But at each place he visited he received the same answer, that there was no help needed just then.

"This is discouraging," he told himself, as he retired that night. "Perhaps I'll have to go to the country or back to Riverside after all."

Yet he was up bright and early the next day and just as eager as ever to obtain a situation.

He had heard of a new hotel called the Grandon House and visited it directly after breakfast.

As he entered the corridor he heard his name called and turning around saw Andrew Mallison.

"How do you do, Mr. Mallison," said our hero, shaking hands. "I didn't expect to meet you here."

"I've got a little special business in Philadelphia," said the hotel man. "I came in last night and I am going back this afternoon. How are you making out?"

"It's all out so far," and Joe smiled faintly at his own joke.

"No situation, eh?"

"That's it."

"Why don't you strike the people here. It's a new place and the proprietor may need help."

"That is what I came for."

"I'll put in a good word for you, Joe. Come on."

Andrew Mallison led the way to the office and called up a stout, pleasant looking man.

"Mr. Drew, this is a young friend of mine, Joe Bodley. He worked for me this summer, - around the boats and also in the hotel. Now that the season is at an end he is trying to find something to do in the city. If you have an opening I can recommend him."

Mr. Arthur Drew surveyed Joe critically. The new hotel was to be run in first-class style and he wanted his help to be of the best. He rather liked Joe's appearance and he took note of the fact that our hero's hands were scrupulously clean and that his shoes were blacked.

"I've got almost all the help I need, but I might take him on," he said, slowly. "One of my present boys does not suit me at all. He is too impudent."

"Well, Joe is never impudent and he is very reliable," answered Andrew Mallison.

"I'll give you a trial."

"Thank you, sir."

"The wages will depend upon whether you board here or outside."

"How much will you give me if I stay at the hotel?"

"Four dollars a week."

"And what if I board outside?"

"Nine dollars a week."

"Can you give the boy a pretty fair room?" asked Andrew Mallison. "I know yo'll like him after he has been here a while."

"He can have a room with another boy. That lad yonder," and the proprietor of the Grandon House pointed with his hand.

Joe looked and saw that the other lad was gentlemanly looking and rather pleasant.

"It will suit me to stay here, I think," he said. "Anyway, I am willing to try it."

"When can you come to work?"

"Right away - or at least, as soon as I can get my suit case from where I have been stopping."

"Then come in after dinner and I'll tell you what to do and turn you over to my head man. Randolph, come here!"

At the call a bell boy came up.

"This is another boy who is to work here," said Arthur Drew. He will room with you."

"Thank you, Mr. Drew, I'll be glad to get rid of Jack Sagger," said Frank Randolph.

"What's your name?" he went on to our hero.

"Joe Bodley."

"Mine is Frank Randolph. I guess we'll get along all right."

"I hope so, Frank," said Joe, and shook hands.

There was a little more talk and then Joe left, to get his dress suit case and a few other things which belonged to him. By one o'clock he was back to the Grandon House, and just in time to see Andrew Mallison going away.

"I am much obliged, Mr. Mallison, for what you have done," said our hero, warmly.

"You're welcome, Joe," answered the hotel man. "I take an interest in you and I trust you do well here."

"I shall do my best."

After Andrew Mallison had gone Joe was shown around the hotel and instructed in his various duties. Occasionally he was to do bell-boy duty, but usually he was to be an all-around helper for the office.

"I think you'll like it here," said Frank Randolph. "It's the best hotel I've ever worked in. Mr. Drew is a perfect gentleman."

"I am glad to hear it, Frank," answered our hero.

The room assigned to the two boys was a small one on the top floor of the hotel. But it was clean, contained two nice cots, and Joe felt it would suit him very well. Frank had hung up a few pictures and had a shelf full of books and this made the apartment look quite home-like.

"I'm going to buy some books myself, this winter," said Joe. "And when I get time I am going to do some studying."

"I'm studying myself, Joe. I never had much schooling," returned Frank.

"Are you alone in the world?"

"No, my father is living. But he is rather sickly and lives with an uncle of mine, over in Camden. He can't work very much, and that is why I have to support myself. Are you alone?"

"Yes. I think my father is living but I can't locate him."

The next day and for several days following Joe pitched into work in earnest. Many things were strange to him, but he determined to master them as speedily as possible, and this pleased Arthur Drew.

Horatio Alger Jr.

"That boy is all right," he said to his cashier. "I am glad that Andrew Mallison brought him to me."

"Jack Sagger was awfully angry at being discharged," said the cashier.

"It was his own fault. I cannot afford to have a boy around who is impudent."

What the cashier said about the discharged lad was true. Jack Sagger was "mad clear through," and he attributed his discharge solely to Joe.

"I'll fix dat pill," he said to one of his chums. "He ain't going to do me out of my job an' not suffer fer it."

"What are you going to do, Jack?" asked the companion.

"I'll mash him, dat's wot I'll do," answered Jack Sagger.

He was a big, rawboned lad, several inches taller than Joe. His face was freckled, and his lips discolored by cigarette smoking. He was a thoroughly tough boy and it was a wonder that he had ever been allowed to work in the hotel at all. He had a fairly good home, but only went there to sleep and to get his meals.

"Joe, I hear that Jack Sagger is going to make it warm for you," said Frank, one Monday afternoon.

"I suppose he is angry because I got his position, is that it?"

"Yes."

"What is he going to do?"

"I don't know exactly, but he'll hurt you if he can."

"If he attacks me I'll do what I can to take care of myself," answered our hero.

That afternoon he was sent out by Mr. Drew on an errand that took him to a neighborhood occupied largely by wholesale provision houses. As Joe left the hotel Jack Sagger saw him.

"Dere's dat country jay now," said Sagger.

"Now's your time to git square on him, Jack," said Nick Sammel, his crony.

"Right you are, Nick. Come on."

"Going to follow him?"

"Yes, till I git him where I want him."

"Going to mash him?"

"Sure. When I git through wid him his own mother won't know him," went on Jack Sagger, boastfully.

"Maybe he'll git the cops after you, Jack."

"I'll watch out fer dat, Nick, an' you must watch out too," answered Jack Sagger.

"Are you sure you kin best him? He looks putty strong."

"Huh! Can't I fight? Didn't I best Sam Nolan, and Jerry Dibble?"

"That's right, Jack."

"Just let me git one chanct at him an' he'll run away, you see if he don't. But he shan't git away until I give him a black eye an' knock out a couple of his front teeth fer him," concluded the boaster.

CHAPTER XVIII.

JOE SHOWS HIS MUSCLE.

All unconscious that he was being followed, our hero went on his errand to a wholesale provision house that supplied the Grandon Hotel with meats and poultry. He felt in good spirits and so whistled lightly as he walked.

Arriving at the place of business he transacted his errand as speedily as possible and then started to return to the hotel.

He was just passing the entrance to a factory yard when he felt a hand on his shoulder, and wheeling around found himself confronted by Jack Sagger, Nick Sammel, and half a dozen others, who had gathered to see their leader "polish off" the country boy.

"What do you want?" demanded Joe, sharply.

"You know well enough wot I want, country!" exclaimed Jack Sagger.

"I do not."

"You took my job away from me, an' I'm goin' to pay you fer doing it."

"Mr. Drew had a perfect right to discharge you, Jack Sagger. He said you were impudent and he didn't want you around any more."

"You can't preach to me, country! Do you know wot I'm goin' ter do?"

"No."

"I'm going to make you promise to leave dat job. Will yer promise?"

"No."

"Den you have got to fight," and Jack Sagger began to pull up his rather dirty coat sleeves.

"Supposing I don't want to fight?" went on our hero, as calmly as he could.

"Yer got ter do it, country - or else make dat promise."

"I'll make no promise to you."

"Den take dat!"

As Jack Sagger uttered the last words he launched a blow at Joe's nose. But our hero ducked and the blow went wide of its mark.

"Give it to him, Jack!"

"Show him what you can do!"

"Keep off," came from Joe. "If you don't, you'll get hurt!"

"Hear dat now! Jack, pitch in, quick, before anybody comes!"

Thus urged Jack Sagger struck out once more, landing on Joe's chest. Then our hero drew back and sent in a blow with all his force. It took the other boy squarely on the chin and sent him staggering against a friend.

If ever there was a surprised boy that boy was Jack Sagger. He had expected that to "polish off" Joe would be easy and he had not anticipated such a defense as had been made. He righted himself and gazed stupidly at our hero.

"Wot did yer hit me fer?" he gasped.

"You keep off or I'll hit you again," answered Joe.

There was a pause and Sagger sprang forward, trying to catch Joe around the arms. But our hero was too quick for him and ducked once more. Then he hit the bully in the ear and gave him another blow in the left eye.

"Ouch!" roared Jack Sagger. "Don't! Oh, my eye!"

"Have you had enough?" demanded Joe, who was commencing to warm up.

"Pitch in, fellers!" came from Jack Sagger. "Throw him down!"

"Ain't you going to do it alone?" queried Nick Sammel, in wonder, not unmingled with a suspicion that Joe would not be as easy to handle as anticipated.

"I - I've got a - a heartburn," came lamely from Sagger. "It come on me all at onct. If it wasn't fer that I'd do him up all alone."

"You're a fraud, and you haven't any heart-burn!" cried Joe. "You're afraid, that's all. If you want to fight, stand up, and we'll have it out."

"Don't you call me afraid," said Sagger, but his voice had lost much of its bullying tone.

"You're a big coward, Jack Sagger. After this I want you to leave me alone."

"Ain't you fellers going to pitch in?" demanded Sagger, turning to his cohorts.

"The first boy to hit me will get paid back with interest," said Joe, sharply. "I don't like to fight but I can do it if I have to."

One or two had edged forward but when they saw his determined air they slunk back.

"Go on and fight him, Jack," said one. "This is your mix-up, not ours."

"You said you was going to do him up brown," put in another.

"Ain't I got the heartburn?" blustered the bully. "I can't do nuthin' when I git that. Wait till I'm well; then I'll show him."

"If you ever touch me again, Jack Sagger, I'll give you the worst thrashing you ever had," said Joe, loudly.

"Remember, I am not the least bit afraid of you. The best thing you can do is to keep your distance."

"Humph!"

"I don't want to quarrel with anybody, but I am always ready to stick up for my rights, just you remember that."

So speaking Joe backed out of the crowd, that opened to let him pass. Several of the boys wanted to detain him, but not one had the courage to do so. As soon as he was clear of his tormentors, he hurried back to the hotel.

"How did you make out?" asked Mr. Drew.

"It's all right, sir, and they'll send the things to-night, sure," answered Joe. He hestitated for a moment. "I had a little excitement on the way."

"How was that?"

"Jack Sagger and some other boys followed me up and wanted to polish me off."

"You don't look as if they had done much polishing." And the hotel man smiled.

"No, Jack Sagger got the worst of it. I guess he'll leave me alone in the future."

"You mustn't fight around the hotel, Joe."

"This was on the way to Jackson & Bell's, sir. I was bound to defend myself."

"To be sure. Sagger came to me yesterday and wanted to be taken back, but I told him no - that I wouldn't have such an impudent fellow around."

As the winter season came on the hotel began to fill up and Joe was kept busy from early in the morning until late at night, and so was Frank Randolph. The two boys were firm friends, and on Sunday went to Sunday School together and also to church, when their hotel duties permitted of it.

In the corridor of the hotel Joe, one day, met the timid Felix Gussing, the young man who had once had so much trouble in driving a horse.

"How do you do, Mr. Gussing," said our hero politely.

"Why if it isn't Joe!" cried the young man, and smiled. "What are you doing here?"

"I work at this hotel now."

"Is it possible! Didn't you like it at Riverside?"

"Yes, but the place is shut up for the winter."

"Ah, I see."

"Are you stopping here, sir?"

"Yes, I came in an hour ago. I have business in Philadelphia."

"Maybe you're buying horses," said Joe, slyly.

"No! no! No more horses for me," ejaculated the dude.

"I - er - this is of more importance."

No more was said just then, but later our hero met Felix Gussing again, and on the day following had an errand that took him to the young man's room.

"Joe, you are quite a wise boy, perhaps I can confide in you," said Felix Gussing, after some talk on other subjects.

"I'll be glad to be of service to you, Mr. Gussing."

"I have a delicate problem to solve. Sometimes a young man can give better advice than an older person," went on the dude.

"Don't flatter me, Mr. Gussing."

"I am in love," went on the young man, flatly.

"Yes, sir."

"I am quite sure the young lady loves me."

"Then I suppose you are going to get married."

"There is an obstacle in the way."

"Oh!"

"Perhaps I had better tell you the whole story - if you'll listen to me," went on the dude.

"Certainly I'll listen," said Joe. "I've got a little time off."

And then Felix Gussing told his tale of woe, as will be found in the next chapter.

CHAPTER XIX.

ONE KIND OF A DUEL.

"Her name is Clara, and she is the daughter of Major Thomas Botts Sampson, of the regular army," began Felix Gussing.

"Then her father is a military man."

"Exactly, and that is the trouble," and the dude gave a groan. "It is this way: When I went to see Major Sampson he greeted me very cordially, until I disclosed the object of my visit.

" 'Sir,' said he 'This is a matter which requires consideration. Have you gained my daughter's consent?'

" 'I have,' I answered.

" 'So far so good,' said he. 'But there is one thing more. Have you served in the army?'

" 'No,' said I.

" 'Or fought a duel?'

" 'No.'

Horatio Alger Jr.

"Then he told me to remember that he had served in the army and that his daughter was the daughter of an army man, one who had gone through many battles. After that he said he was resolved that his daughter should marry only somebody who had proved himself a man of courage."

"What did you do then?" asked Joe, becoming interested.

"What could I do? I am - er - no army man - no fighter. Evidently the major wants a fighter for a son-in-law," and Felix Gussing groaned once more.

"You'll have to become a fighter," said Joe.

"No! no! I am a er - a man of peace!" cried the dude, in alarm.

"Mr. Gussing, I think I can arrange matters for you," said Joe, struck by a certain idea.

"What can you mean, Joe?"

"I mean that I can prove to Major Sampson that you are a brave man."

"Do that, Joe, and I shall be your friend for life!" gasped the dude.

"Will you wait until to-morrow, Mr. Gussing?"

"Certainly, but do not keep me in suspense too long."

"This may cost you a little money."

"I don't care if it costs a hundred dollars."

"Then I am sure I can fix it up for you," answered Joe.

There was stopping at the hotel a man named Montgomery. He had at different times been an auctioneer, a book-agent, a schoolmaster, and a traveling salesman. He was just now selling curiosities and Joe felt that he would be only too glad to do Felix Gussing a good turn if he were paid for it.

Our hero had a talk with this man, and the upshot of the matter was that Montgomery and the dude were introduced on the following morning.

"I think I can help you, Mr. Gussing," said the curiosity man, who, it may be mentioned here, was a tall and important-looking personage. "I was once in the army."

"What can you do?" questioned the dude, hopefully.

"Will it be worth fifty dollars to you if I aid you in winning the consent of Major Sampson to wed his daughter?"

"Decidedly."

"This is also Joe's plan, so you will have to pay him, too."

"I don't want any money," put in our hero.

"Joe shall have ten dollars - if your plan wins out. But how is all this to be accomplished?" continued Felix Gussing.

"We will take the earliest possible opportunity to visit Major Sampson," said Ulmer Montgomery.

"Well?"

"When we are all together, we'll get into some sort of an argument. You shall call me a fool and I'll slap you in the face. Then you shall challenge me to a duel."

"A duel! Why, sir, I - er - I never could shoot you, and I don't want to be shot myself."

"My dear Mr. Gussing, you don't understand me. Don't you comprehend, the pistols shall be loaded with powder only."

"Ah, that's the idea!" exclaimed the dude, much relieved.

"Yes. You see it will only be a sham duel so far as we are concerned, but will, in the most harmless fashion possible, prove you to be a man of honor and courage. Major Sampson's scruples will vanish, and you will have the pleasure of gaining his daughter's hand in marriage.

"I agree, Mr. Montgomery - the plan is a famous one. Is it yours or is it Joe's?"

"Joe's - but it will fall to me to help carry it out," said the Jack-of-all-trades, who did not lose sight of the fifty dollars that had been promised to him.

On the following day Felix Gussing and Mr. Montgomery took themselves to Major Sampson's residence, where the stranger was introduced as a curiosity hunter from Chicago.

"He wishes to look at your collection of swords," said the dude.

"I shall be delighted to show them," said the major, who was a person of great self-importance.

"Ah, this is a fine sword from the Holy Land," said Mr. Montgomery, handling one of the blades.

"I don't know where it came from," said the major. "It was presented to me by a friend from Boston."

"That is a Russian sword," said the dude. "I know it by its handle."

"That sword is from the Holy Land," insisted Mr. Montgomery.

"Anybody is a fool to talk that way," cried Felix Gussing.

"Ha! do you call me a fool, sir!" stormed Montgomery.

"Gentlemen!" put in the major. "I think -"

"I am not a fool, sir, and I want you to know it!" bellowed Ulmer Montgomery. "It's an outrage to call me such. Take that, sir!" and he slapped Felix Gussing lightly on the cheek.

"Gentlemen, this must cease!" cried the major, coming between them. "In my house, too! Disgraceful!"

"He has got to apologize to me!" roared the dude,

acting his part to perfection.

"Never!" shouted Montgomery.

"If you will not, I demand satisfaction. I - I will fight you in a duel."

"A duel!"

"Yes, a duel. Pistols, at ten paces," went on Felix Gussing.

"Well! well!" came from the major in amazement.

"Can I do less?" demanded the would-be son-in-law. "My honor is at stake."

"Then stand by your honor by all means," cried the military man, who, at times, was as hot-blooded as anybody.

During the talk the major's daughter had come upon the scene.

"Oh, Felix, what does this mean?" she demanded.

"I am going to fight this - this fellow a duel, pistols at ten paces," answered Felix, firmly.

"Felix!" she gasped. "You will not, you cannot fight. For my sake, do not."

"Clara," answered the dude, smiling affectionately upon her. "For your sake I would forego any personal gratification, but I must not suffer a stain upon the honor."

"Well said!" exclaimed the major. "Felix is behaving well. I couldn't have done better myself. I admire his courage and I give him free permission to wed you after the - the -"

"But father, if he should be killed?" faltered the fair Clara.

"Never fear, Clara; all will go well," interposed Felix.

More words followed, but the dude pretended to be stubborn and so did Ulmer Montgomery. Both went off to arrange about the duel, and the major insisted upon it that he must be on hand to see the affair come off.

Matters were hurried along with all speed, and it was arranged that the duel should take place on the following morning at ten o'clock, in a country spot just outside of the city. Joe was invited to go along, and carried the pistols, and two others were let into the secret, including a doctor, who went fully prepared to attend to any wounds that might be inflicted.

It did not take long to load the pistols, with powder only. Great care was taken so that Major Sampson should not suspect the truth.

"Major," said Felix, in a trembling voice. "If I - if anything serious happens to me tell Clara that - that I died like a man."

"Noble boy! I will! I will!" answered the military man.

"When I give the word, gentlemen, you will both fire!" said one of the seconds.

"Very well," answered both of the duelists.

"Ready? One - two - three - fire!"

Both pistols were simultaneously discharged. When the smoke cleared away it was ascertained that both parties were unharmed.

"Gentlemen, are you satisfied?" asked the seconds.

"I am," answered Ulmer Montgomery, quickly.

"Then I shall be," put in Felix Gussing. "And now that this affair is at an end, Mr. Montgomery will you shake hands?" he added.

"With pleasure, Mr. Gussing!" was the reply. "I must say in all frankness I am sorry we quarrelled in the first place. Perhaps I was wrong about the sword."

"And perhaps I was wrong."

"Both of you were wrong," put in the major. "I hunted up the letter that came with the blade. It is an old Spanish weapon. Let us all call the affair off, and Mr. Montgomery shall come to Clara's wedding to Mr. Gussing."

"With all my heart," cried Montgomery, and there the little plot came to a finish.

CHAPTER XX.

ATTACKED IN THE DARK.

"Joe, the plot worked to perfection!" said Felix Gussing, on the day following. "I have to thank you, and here are twenty dollars for your trouble."

"I don't want a cent, Mr. Gussing," answered our hero. "I did it only out of friendliness to you. I hope you have no further trouble in your courtship."

"Oh, that was all settled last night. Clara and I are to be married next week. We are going to send out the cards to-day. You see," went on the young man in a lower tone. "I don't want to give the major a chance to change his mind, or to suspect that that duel was not just what it ought to have been."

"Does he suspect anything as yet?"

"Not a thing."

"Then you are wise to have the wedding as quickly as possible."

"When we are married I am going to let Clara into the secret. I know she'll enjoy it as much as anybody."

Horatio Alger Jr.

"Well, you had better warn her to keep mum before her father. He looks as if he could get pretty angry if he wanted to."

"As you won't take any money for this, Joe, wouldn't you like to come to the wedding?"

"I'm afraid it will be too high-toned for me, Mr. Gussing."

"No, it is to be a plain, homelike affair - Clara wants it that way. The major has some country cousins who will be there, and they are very plain folks."

"Then I'll come - if Miss Sampson wishes it."

So it was arranged that Joe should attend the wedding, and as he was in need of a new Sunday suit he purchased it at once, so that he could use it at the wedding.

"You're in luck, Joe," remarked Frank, when he heard the news. "And that suit looks very well on you."

In some manner it leaked out among the boys that Joe was going to the wedding, and two days before the affair came off Jack Sagger learned of it. He immediately consulted with some of his cronies, and it was unanimously resolved to watch for Joe after the wedding was over and chastise him severely for the manner in which he had treated "the gang."

"We'll fix him," said Sagger, suggestively.

At the proper time Joe took a car to the Sampson home and was there introduced to a dozen or more people.

The wedding proved an enjoyable affair and the elegant supper that was served was one long to be remembered.

It was nearly eleven o'clock when Joe started for the hotel again. He had thought to take a car, but afterwards concluded to walk.

"A walk will do me good - after such a hearty supper," he told himself. "If I ride home I won't be able to sleep."

At the corner the Sagger crowd was waiting for him. One gave a low whistle, and all slunk out of sight until Joe had passed.

Several blocks had been covered when our hero came to a spot where several new buildings were in the course of construction. It was rather dark and the street lights cast long and uncertain shadows along the walk.

Joe had just started to cross a wooden bridge over an excavation when he heard a rush behind him. Before he could turn he was given a violent shove.

"Push him into de cellar hole!" came, in Jack Sagger's voice.

"Stop!" cried Joe, and it must be admitted that he was greatly alarmed. But no attention was paid to his words, and over the side of the bridge he went, to fall a distance of a dozen feet and land in a pile of dirt, with one lower limb in a puddle of dirty water.

"Down he goes!" he heard, in the voice of Nick Sammel. "Wonder how he likes it?"

　　　　　Horatio Alger Jr.

"You're a mean, low crowd!" cried Joe, as he stood up. He was covered with dirt and the cold water felt anything but agreeable on such a frosty night as it chanced to be.

"Don't you dare to crawl out of dat!" said Sagger. "If yer do we'll pitch yer in ag'in, won't we, fellers?"

"Sure we will!" was the cry.

"De next time we'll dump him in on his head!"

Growing somewhat accustomed to the semi-darkness, Joe counted seven of his tormentors, all standing on the edge of the cellar hole into which he had so unceremoniously been thrown. Several of the youths had heavy sticks.

"I suppose I'll have to retreat," he reasoned "I can't fight seven of them."

He turned to the rear of the cellar hole and felt his way along into the deepest shadows. Presently he reached a partly finished building and crawled up some planks leading to one of the floors.

"He is running away!" he heard Jack Sagger cry.

"Come on after him!" said another of the crowd.

"Let's take his new coat and vest away from him!" added a third.

The entire party dropped down into the hole and ran to the rear, in a hunt after our hero. In the meantime Joe was feeling his way along a scaffolding where some masons had been at work.

As it happened the entire party under Jack Sagger walked toward the unfinished building and came to a halt directly under the scaffolding. Joe saw them and crouched back out of sight.

"Where is de country jay?" he heard one of the crowd ask.

"He's back here somewhere," answered Jack Sagger. "We must find him an' thump him good."

"You'll not thump me if I can help it," said our hero to himself.

Joe put out his hand and felt a cask near by. It was half filled with dirty water, being used for the purposes of making mortar. A tub of water was beside the cask.

"Tit for tat!" he thought, and as quickly as it could be done he overturned the cask and the tub followed.

Joe's aim was perfect, and down came the shower of dirty water, directly on the heads of the boys below. Every one was saturated and each set up a yell of dismay.

"Oh, say, I'm soaked!"

"He trun water all over me!"

"Ugh! but dat's a regular ice bath, dat is!"

"That's what you get for throwing me into the hole!" cried Joe. "After this you had better leave me alone."

"I've got some mortar in me eye!" screamed Jack Sagger, dancing around in pain. "Oh, me eye is burned out!"

"I'm wet to de skin!" said Nick Sammel, with a shiver. "Oh, say, but it's dead cold, ain't it?"

Waiting to hear no more, Joe ran along the scaffolding and then leaped through a window of the unfinished building. A street light now guided him and he came out through the back of the structure and into an alleyway. From this he made his way to the street.

"I'll have to hurry," he reasoned. "If they catch me now they will want to half kill me!"

"Don't let him git away!" he heard Sagger roar. "Catch him! Catch him!"

"Hold on there, you young rascals!" came a voice out of the darkness. "What are you doing around these buildings?"

A watchman had come on the scene, with a lantern in one hand and a heavy club in the other.

"We ain't doin' nuthin," said one of the boys.

"Maybe you're the gang that stole that lumber a couple of nights ago," went on the watchman, coming closer.

"Ain't touched yer lumber," growled Jack Sagger.

"We're after anudder feller wot hid in here," said Sammel.

"That's a likely story. I believe you are nothing but a crowd of young thieves," grumbled the watchman. "Every night somebody is trying to steal lumber or bricks, or something. I've a good mind to make an example of you and have you all locked up."

"We ain't touched a thing!" cried a small boy, and began to back away in alarm. At once several followed him.

"Here's a barrel of water knocked over and everything in a mess. You've been skylarking, too. I'm going to have you locked up!"

The watchman made a dash after the boys and the crowd scattered in all directions. Sagger received a crack on the shoulder that lamed him for a week, and Sammel tripped and went down, taking the skin off of the end of his nose.

"Oh, me nose!" he moaned. "It's busted entirely!"

"Run!" cried Sagger. "If you don't you'll be nabbed sure!" And then the crowd ran with all their speed, scrambling out of the hole as best they could. They did not stop until they were half a dozen blocks away and on their way home.

"We made a fizzle of it dat trip," said Sagger, dolefully.

"It's all your fault," growled one of the boys. "I ain't goin' out wid you again. You promise big things but you never do 'em."

"Oh, Jack's a gas-bag, dat's wot he is," was the

comment of another, and he walked off by himself. Presently one after another of the boys followed suit, leaving Jack Sagger to sneak home, a sadder if not a wiser lad.

CHAPTER XXI.

DAYS AT THE HOTEL.

"Perhaps those fellows have learned a lesson they won't forget in a hurry," remarked Frank to Joe, after he learned the particulars of the attack in the dark.

"I hope they don't molest me further," answered our hero. "If they'll only let me alone I'll let them alone."

"That Sagger is certainly on the downward path," said Frank. "If he doesn't look out he'll land in jail."

What Frank said was true, and less than a week later they heard through another hotel boy that Jack Sagger had been arrested for stealing some lead pipe out of a vacant residence. The pipe had been sold to a junkman for thirty cents and the boy had spent the proceeds on a ticket for a cheap theater and some cigarettes. He was sent to the House of Correction, and that was the last Joe heard of him.

With the coming of winter the hotel filled up and Joe was kept busy from morning to night, so that he had little time for studying. He performed his duties faithfully and the hotel proprietor was much pleased in consequence.

Horatio Alger Jr.

"Joe is all right," he said to his cashier, "I can trust him with anything."

"That's so, and he is very gentlemanly, too," replied the cashier.

Ulmer Montgomery was still at the hotel. He was now selling antiquaries, and our hero often watched the fellow with interest. He suspected that Montgomery was a good deal of a humbug, but could not prove it.

At length Montgomery told Joe that he was going to the far West to try his fortunes. The man seemed to like our hero, and the night before he left the hotel he called Joe into his room.

"I want to make you a present of some books I own," said Ulmer Montgomery. "Perhaps you'll like to read them. They are historical works."

"Thank you, Mr. Montgomery, you are very kind."

"I used to be a book agent, but I gave that up as it didn't pay me as well as some other things."

"And you had these books left over?"

"Yes. The firm I worked for wouldn't take them back so I had to keep them."

"And now you are selling curiosities."

At this Ulmer Montgomery smiled blandly.

"Not exactly, Joe - I only sell curiosities, or antiquities, when I am hard up. On other occasions I do like other folks, work for a living."

"I don't quite understand."

"I dropped into selling curiosities when I was in the South and hard up for cash. I wanted money the worst way, and I - well, I set to work to raise it. Maybe you'd like to hear my story."

"I would."

"Mind you, I don't pose as a model of goodness and I shouldn't advise you to follow in my footsteps. But I wanted money and wanted in badly. So I put on my thinking cap, and I soon learned of a very zealous antiquary living about five miles from where I was stopping. He was wealthy and a bachelor, and spent no inconsiderable portion of his income on curiosities."

"And you went to him?" said Joe, becoming interested.

"I at once determined to take advantage of this gentleman's antiquarian zeal. I will own that I had some qualms of conscience - about imposing upon the old gentleman, but I didn't know of any other way to procure the money I absolutely needed.

"Having made all of my preparations, I set off for Mr. Leland's house. To disguise myself I put on a pair of big goggles and an old-fashioned collar and tie.

" 'I understand, Mr. Leland, that you are in the habit of collecting curiosities,' I said.

" 'Quite right, sir,' said he. 'I have got together some few,' and he gazed with an air of pride at the nondescript medley which surrounded him.

" 'I have in my possession,' I proceeded, 'two or three of great value, which I had hoped to retain, but, well, I need money, and so I must part with them, much as I wish to call them mine. But I wish to see that they get into the proper hands, and I have been told that you are a great antiquarian, understanding the true value of such things, and so - '

" 'Pray, show them to me at once!' cried the old man, eagerly.

" 'I have traveled a good deal, and been a pilgrim in many climes,' I went on. 'I have wandered along the banks of the Euphrates and dipped my feet in the currents of the Nile. I have gazed upon ruined cities - '

" 'Yes! yes! show me what you have!' he cried, eagerly.

" 'Here is a curiosity of the highest order', I said, opening a paper and showing a bit of salt about the size of a walnut. 'This is a portion of the statue of salt into which Lot's wife was turned.'

" 'Is it possible?' cried the antiquary, taking the salt and gazing at it in deep veneration. 'Are you quite certain of this?'

" 'I am,' I answered. 'It is a portion of the wrist. I broke it off myself. The hand was already gone.' "

"And did he buy it?" questioned Joe, in astonishment.

"He did, and gave me fifty dollars in cash for it."

"But that wasn't fair, Mr. Montgomery."

The seller of bogus curiosities shrugged his shoulders.

"Perhaps not. But I was hard up and had to do something."

"Did you sell him anything else?"

"I did - a walking stick, which I had procured in Connecticut. It was covered with strange carvings and he mistook them for hieroglyphics, and gave me ten dollars for the thing."

"I don't see how you could have the nerve to do such things, Mr. Montgomery."

"Well, a man can do lots of things when he is driven to do them. I admit the deals were rather barefaced, but, as I said before, I had to do something. Some day, when I am rich, I'll return the money to the old fellow," added the impostor.

He left the hotel that morning, and it may be said here that Joe did not meet him again for several years.

Christmas came and went at the hotel, and our hero received several presents from his friends, including a pair of gloves from Ned Talmadge and a five-dollar gold piece from Felix Gussing. Some of the regular boarders at the hotel also remembered him.

"And how do you like married life?" asked Joe, of Felix Gussing.

"We are getting along very nicely," said the dude.

"Have you told your wife about the duel yet?"

"No, - and I don't think I shall," added Felix Gussing. "You see she - er - she thinks me a very brave man and - "

"And you don't want her to change her opinion," finished Joe, with a smile!

"Why should I, Joe."

"Oh, I don't know as there is any reason, excepting that they usually say men and their wives should have no secrets from each other."

"Mr. Montgomery is gone, I see," said the dude, changing the subject.

"Yes, sir."

"Then you are the only one who knows of this secret. You won't tell, will you?"

"No, sir."

"We are having troubles enough as it is," went on the dude. "Both my wife and I find housekeeping rather troublesome. It is hard to obtain proper servants, and she does not care to do the work herself."

"Why don't you go to boarding?"

"Perhaps we will, later on."

With the new year came a heavy fall of snow and soon sleighs big and little were in demand. Then came a slight fall of rain which made the sidewalks a glare of ice.

"Got to be careful," announced Frank to Joe. "If you don't you'll go down on your back."

"I intend to be careful," answered our hero. "I have no wish to break any bones."

That afternoon Joe was sent on an errand to a place of business half a mile away. On returning he chanced to stop at a street corner, to watch a number of children who had made a long slide for themselves.

As he stood watching, a man came along bundled up in a great coat and wearing a slouch hat and blue glasses. The man was walking rapidly, as if in a hurry.

"That fellow looks familiar to me," thought Joe. "Wonder who he can be?"

He watched the stranger cross the street. Then the fellow happened to step on the icy slide and in a twinkling he went down on his back, his hat flying in one direction and a bundle he carried in another.

"Hurrah! Down goes the gent!" sang out a newsboy standing near.

"Come here an' I'll pick yer up!" said another street urchin.

"You rascals, you fixed this on purpose so I should fall!" cried the man, starting to get up.

"Can I help you?" questioned Joe, coming up, and then

he gave a start, as he recognized the fellow.

It was Pat Malone, alias David Ball, from Montana!

CHAPTER XXII.

ABOUT SOME MINING SHARES.

"How do you do, Mr. Ball?" said our hero, coolly.

"Eh, what's that?" questioned Malone, in amazement. Then he recognized Joe, and his face fell.

"I have often wondered what became of you," went on our hero. "Let me help you up."

"I - that is - who are you, boy?" demanded Malone, getting to his feet and picking up his hat and his bundle.

"You ought to remember me. I am Joe Bodley. I used to work for Mr. Mallison, at Riverside."

"Don't know the man or the place," said Pat Malone, coolly. "You have made a mistake."

"Then perhaps I had better call you Malone."

"Not at all. My name is Fry - John Fry."

"How often do you change your name, Mr. Fry."

"Don't get impudent!"

"I am not impudent, - I am only asking a plain question."

"I never change my name."

At that moment Joe saw a policeman on the opposite side of the street and beckoned for the officer to come over.

"Hi! what's the meaning of this!" ejaculated Pat Malone.

"Officer, I want this man locked up," said Joe, and caught the rascal by the arm, that he might not run away.

"What's the charge?" asked the bluecoat.

"He is wanted for swindling."

"Boy, are you really crazy?"

"No, I am not."

"Who are you?" asked the policeman, eyeing Joe sharply.

"My name is Joe Bodley. I work at the Grandon House. I will make a charge against this man, and I'll bring the man who was swindled, too."

"That's fair talk," said the policeman. "I guess you'll both have to go to the station with me."

"I'm willing," said Joe, promptly.

"I - I cannot go - I have a sick wife - I must get a doctor," stammered Pat Malone. "Let me go. The boy is mistaken."

"You'll have to go with me."

"But my sick wife?"

"You can send for your friends and they can take care of her."

"I have no friends - we are strangers in Philadelphia. I don't want to go."

Pat Malone tried to move on, but the policeman and Joe detained him, and in the end he was marched off to the police station. Here Joe told what he knew and Malone's record was looked up in the Rogues' Gallery.

"You've got the right man, that's sure," said the desk sergeant to our hero. "Now where can you find this Mr. Maurice Vane?"

"I have his address at the hotel," answered our hero. "If I can go I'll get it and send Mr. Vane a telegram."

"Bring the address here and we'll communicate with Mr. Vane."

Our hero agreed, and inside of half an hour a message was sent to Maurice Vane, notifying him of the fact that Pat Malone had been caught. Mr. Vane had gone to New York on business, but came back to Philadelphia the next day.

When he saw that he was caught Pat Malone broke

down utterly and made a full confession, telling in detail how the plot against Maurice Vane had been carried out.

"It was not my plan," said he. "Gaff Caven got the mining shares and he arranged the whole thing."

"Where did you get the shares - steal them?" demanded Maurice Vane, sharply.

"No, we didn't steal them. We bought them from an old miner for fifty dollars. The miner is dead now."

"Can you prove this?"

"Yes."

"Then do so."

"Why?"

"I don't care to answer that question. But if you can prove to me that you and Caven came by those shares honestly I won't prosecute you, Malone."

"I will prove it!" was the quick answer, and that very afternoon Pat Malone proved beyond a doubt that the shares had belonged to himself and Gaff Caven when they sold them to Maurice Vane.

"That is all I want of you," said Maurice Vane. "I shan't appear against you, Malone."

"Then those shares must be valuable after all?" queried the swindler.

"Perhaps they are. I am having them looked up. I am glad of this opportunity of proving that they are now my absolute property."

"If Caven and I sold you good stocks we ought to be kicked full of holes," grumbled Malone.

"That was your lookout, not mine," returned Maurice Vane. "Mind, I don't say the shares are valuable. But they may be, and if so I shall be satisfied with my bargain."

"Humph! where do I come in?"

"You don't come in at all - and you don't deserve to."

"If I didn't swindle you, you can't have me held for swindling."

"I don't intend to have you held. You can go for all I care."

Maurice Vane explained the situation to the police authorities and that evening Pat Malone was allowed to go. He threatened to have somebody sued for false imprisonment but the police laughed at him.

"Better not try it on, Malone," said one officer. "Remember, your picture is in our Rogues' Gallery," and then the rascal was glad enough to sneak away. The next day he took a train to Baltimore, where, after an hour's hunt, he found Gaff Caven.

"We made a fine mess of things," he said, bitterly. "A fine mess!"

"What are you talking about, Pat?" asked Caven.

"Do you remember the mining stocks we sold to Maurice Vane?"

"Certainly I do."

"Well, he has got 'em yet."

"All right, he can keep them. We have his money too," and Gaff Caven chuckled.

"I'd rather have the shares."

"Eh?"

"I said I'd rather have the shares, Gaff. We put our foot into it when we sold 'em."

"Do you mean to say the shares are valuable?" demanded Gaff Caven.

"That's the size of it."

"Who told you this?"

"Nobody told me, but I can put two and two together as quick as anybody."

"Well, explain."

"I was in Philadelphia when I ran into that hotel boy, Joe Bodley."

"What of that?"

"He had me arrested. Then they sent for Mr. Maurice Vane, and Vane made me prove that the shares were really ours when we sold them to him. I thought I'd go clear if I could prove that, so I went and did it. Then Vane said he wouldn't prosecute me, for the shares might be valuable after all."

"But the mine is abandoned."

"Maybe it is and maybe it isn't. I guess Mr. Maurice Vane knows what he is doing, and we were fools to sell out to him."

"If that mine is valuable I'm going to have it!" cried Gaff Caven. "He can have his money back!" and the rascal who had overreached himself began to pace the floor.

"Maybe he won't take his money back."

"Then I'll claim the mine anyway, Pat - and you must help me."

"What can you do?"

"Go out to Montana, just as soon as the weather is fit, and relocate the mine. If it's any good we can find some fellows to help us hold it somehow. I'm not going to let this slip into Maurice Vane's hands without a struggle."

"Talk is cheap, but it takes money to pay for railroad tickets," went on Malone.

"I've got the dust, Pat."

"Enough to fight Vane off if he should come West?"

"I think so. I met a rich fellow last week and I got a loan of four thousand dollars."

"Without security?" and Malone winked suggestively.

"Exactly. Oh, he was a rich find," answered Gaff Caven, and gave a short laugh.

"I'm willing to go anywhere. I'm tired of things here. It's getting too warm for comfort."

"Then let us start West next week - after I can finish up a little business here."

"I am willing."

And so the two rascals arranged to do Maurice Vane out of what had become his lawful property.

CHAPTER XXIII.

THE FIRE AT THE HOTEL.

On the day following the scene at the police station Maurice Vane stopped at the Grandon House to interview our hero.

"I must thank you for the interest you have taken in this matter, Joe," said he. "It is not every lad who would put himself out to such an extent."

"I wanted to see justice done, Mr. Vane," answered our hero, modestly.

"Things have taken a sudden change since I saw you last summer," went on Maurice Vane. "Perhaps it will be as well if I tell my whole story."

"I'd like first rate to hear it."

"After I got those shares of stock I felt that I had been swindled, and I was very anxious to get hold of the rascals. But as time went on and I could not locate them I resolved to look into the deal a little more minutely and see if there was any chance of getting my money, or a portion of it, back."

"I should have done the same."

"I wrote to a friend out West and he put me in communication with a mining expert who set to work to find out all about the mine. The expert sent me word, late in the fall, that the mine was, in his opinion, located on a vein of gold well worth working."

"What did you do then?"

"I wanted to go West at once and look into the matter personally, but an aunt died and I had to settle up her estate and see to the care of her two children, and that held me back. Then winter came on, and I knew I'd have to let matters rest until spring."

"Are you going out there in the spring?"

"Yes, - as early as possible, too."

"I hope you find the mine a valuable one, Mr. Vane."

"I place great reliance on what the mining expert said, for he is known as a man who makes no mistakes."

"Then, if the mine proves of value, you'll have gotten a cheap piece of property after all."

"Yes, indeed."

"Won't those swindlers be mad when they hear of this!"

"Most likely, my lad; but they have nobody to blame but themselves. I bought their shares in good faith, while they sold them in bad faith."

"Is your title perfectly clear now?"

"Absolutely so."

"Then I hope the mine proves to be worth millions."

"Thank you, my boy."

"I'd like to own a mine like that myself."

"Would you? Well, perhaps you will some day."

"It's not likely. A hotel boy doesn't earn enough to buy a mine," and our hero laughed.

"If I find the mine worth working and open up for business, how would you like to go out there and work for me?"

"I'd like it very much, Mr. Vane."

"Very well, I'll bear that in mind," answered the possessor of the mining shares.

"Why don't you buy up the rest of the mining shares first?"

"I am going to do so - if I can locate them."

"Perhaps the owners will sell cheap."

"I shall explain the situation and make a fair offer. I do not believe in any underhand work," was the ready answer.

"Then you are not like some men I have met," said Joe, and told about Ulmer Montgomery and his so-called antiquities.

"That man will never amount to anything, Joe - mark my words. He will always be a hanger-on as we call them, in the business world."

"I believe you, sir."

"Honesty pays in the long run. A rogue may make something at the start but sooner or later he will find himself exposed."

Maurice Vane remained at the hotel for a week and then left to go to Chicago on business. From that point he was going to Montana as soon as the weather permitted.

After that several weeks slipped by without anything unusual happening. During those days Joe fell in again with Felix Gussing.

"We are going to move to Riverside," said the dude, if such he may still be called, although he was a good business man. "I have rented a house there - the old Martin place - and if you ever come to the town you must visit us."

"Thank you, I will," answered our hero.

"My wife thinks a great deal of you and you must stop at the house during your stay at Riverside," went on Felix Gussing.

A change came for Joe much quicker than was anticipated. One night, late in the winter, he was just preparing to retire, when he smelt smoke. He ran out of his room and to an air shaft and saw the smoke coming up thickly.

"The hotel must be on fire!" he thought. "If it is, I'll have to notify the management!"

He jumped rather than ran down the several stairways to the hotel office. Here he told the proprietor and the cashier. An examination was made and the fire was located in the laundry.

"Go and awaken all the guests," said Mr. Drew, and Joe ran off to do as bidden. Other boys did the same, and before long the guests were hurrying through the hallways and down the elevators and stairs.

By this time the smoke was coming thickly, and presently a sheet of flame burst through at the rear of the hotel. The fire alarm had been given and several engines and a hook-and-ladder company dashed on the scene.

"Are your guests all out?" demanded a police officer.

"I believe so," answered Mr. Drew.

"I'm going to take a look around," said Joe, and darted upstairs once more.

He visited room after room, only to find them empty. From the rear of the hotel came the crackling of flames and down in the street the fire engines were pounding away, sending their streams of water into the structure.

On the third floor of the building our hero came across an old lady who was rather queer in her mind. The lady was also lame and walked with great difficulty.

"Oh, Joseph! what is the trouble?" she cried.

"The hotel is on fire, Mrs. Dalley. Come, let me help you out."

"On fire! Oh, I must save my canary!" And the old lady started back for her room.

"You haven't got time, Mrs. Dalley. Come with me."

"I cannot let my dear Dick perish!" answered the old lady, firmly.

Joe looked along the hall and saw that the flames were moving swiftly toward the room the old lady had occupied. To enter the apartment would be highly dangerous.

"You simply can't go after the bird, madam," he said. "Come with me!"

"My bird! my bird!" screamed Mrs. Dalley, and tried to run, or rather hobble, towards her room, despite the smoke that was now rolling over her head.

"You must come with me!" exclaimed Joe, and drew her back. She tried to struggle and then, without warning, fainted in his arms.

The burden was a heavy one, but our hero did not shirk the task before him. He half dragged and half carried the unconscious lady to the nearest staircase and almost fell to the bottom.

The smoke on the second floor was so thick he could scarcely see.

But he kept on and went down another flight and

reached the office. He could hardly breathe and the tears were running down both cheeks.

"Hullo there, boy!" came the call of a fireman, as he appeared through the smoke. "Better get out of here!"

"Help me with this lady," answered Joe.

"A lady! Oh, all right!" And in a moment more the fireman had Mrs. Dalley over his shoulder and was carrying her out. Joe came close behind. The lady was taken to a nearby drug store where she speedily revived.

By the prompt efforts of the fire department only a small portion of the hotel was burnt. But the whole building was water-soaked, and all of the boarders had to move out, and then the place was closed up.

"Out of a place once again," thought our hero, rather dismally. "What's to do next?"

This was not an easy question to answer. He looked around for another opening but, finding none, resolved to pay a visit to Riverside.

"I can call on the Gussings, and on Ned," he thought. "I know all of them will be glad to see me. And maybe Mr. Mallison will be wanting to make some arrange-ments for next summer. I suppose he'll run the boats as usual."

"Going to leave Philadelphia, eh?" said Frank. "Do you intend to come back, Joe?"

"I don't know yet, Frank."

"Well, I wish you luck."

"I wish you the same."

"If you go to work for Mallison this summer, maybe you can get me a job too."

"I'll remember that," answered our hero.

His preparations were soon made, and then he boarded a train for Riverside. He did not dream of the surprises in store for him.

CHAPTER XXIV.

THE BLUE BOX AT LAST.

After calling on the Gussings and being invited to remain there for several days, Joe took himself to Ned Talmadge's residence.

Ned was very glad to see him and had to give all the particulars of another trip he had made to the West.

"I had a splendid time," said Ned. "I wish you had been along."

"Then you like the West, Ned?"

"Indeed I do, - better than the East."

"Perhaps I'll go West some day," went on our hero, and told his friend of what Maurice Vane had said.

"I saw some mines while I was out there," continued Ned. "I went to the very bottom of one mine. I can tell you I felt a bit shivery, being so far underground."

"I suppose the miners get used to it."

"It would be a joke on those swindlers if that mine should prove of value," went on Ned, after a pause.

Horatio Alger Jr.

"I hope, for Mr. Vane's sake, it does prove valuable."

"Now your hotel is burnt out, what are you going to do?"

"I haven't made up my mind, Ned. Perhaps I'll come back here, to work for Mr. Mallison."

"Then we'll be together again next summer. That will suit me."

The boys had a good time together and then Joe said he would like to pay a visit to his old home on the mountain side. Ned readily consented to go along.

"But I don't imagine you'll find much of the old cabin left," he added.

There was still a little ice in the lake, but they rowed to the spot without great difficulty and made their way to the tumble-down cabin.

It was not an inviting sight and it made Joe feel sober to view the locality .

"Joe, you never heard anything of that blue box, did you?" asked Ned, after several minutes of silence.

"No."

"It ought to be somewhere in this vicinity."

"It's gone, and that is all there is to it," said our hero, and gave a long sigh.

The boys tramped around the vicinity for a good half

hour, and then sat down on a hollow log to eat a lunch they had brought along.

"Let us build a fire beside the old log," said Ned. "It will help to keep us warm."

Joe was willing and the two boys soon had some leaves and twigs gathered, and placed some good-sized branches on top to make the blaze last. Then they began to eat and to warm themselves at the same time.

"This log would make a good hiding-place for some wild animal," remarked Ned. "Can anything be inside?"

"It's not likely, Ned. The smoke would drive out any living creature."

"I'm going to get a stick and poke into the log."

Both boys procured sticks and began to poke at the log. Presently they felt something move and a half-dazed snake came into view.

"There's your animal, Ned!" exclaimed Joe.

"Oh, a snake! Keep him away!" roared Ned, badly frightened.

"He can't hurt you - he is too stiff from the cold," answered our hero, and quickly dispatched the snake with a stone.

"Do you suppose there are any more in the tree?" asked the rich boy, still keeping at a distance.

"More than likely. I'll poke around with my stick and see."

"Be careful!"

"I am not afraid."

Joe's stick had something of a crotch on the end of it and with this he began to rake among the dead leaves that had blown into the hollow log. He brought out a great quantity but no more snakes showed themselves.

"I reckon he was the only one after all, Ned."

"The log is burning!" said Ned, an instant later. "See, the smoke is coming out of the hollow."

"My stick is caught," said Joe, pulling hard on something. "I guess - well, I declare!"

He gave a jerk, and from the hollow came a square object, covered with smoking dirt and leaves.

"What is it?"

"Unless I am mistaken, it is a tin box."

"Oh, Joe, the blue box?"

Joe did not answer for he was brushing the smoking leaves and dirt from the object. As he cleaned it off he caught sight of some blue paint. On one end the box was badly charred from the fire.

"It's the blue box, sure enough," said Joe.

"And we came close to burning it up!" groaned Ned. "Oh, Joe, I am so sorry!"

"It's not your fault, Ned, I was as much to blame as anybody. But who would look for the box out here?"

"Perhaps some wild animal carried it off."

"That may be."

Joe had the box cleaned off by this time. It was still hot at one end and smoking. He tried to pull it open, but found it locked.

"The contents will burn up before I can open it!" cried Joe.

He did not know what to do, and in desperation began to pry at the box with his stick and his jackknife. Then the box broke open, scattering some half-burnt papers in all directions.

The boys picked the papers up and also a small bag of buckskin. When Joe opened the bag he found it contained exactly a hundred dollars in gold.

"That's a nice find," said Ned. "Anyway, you are a hundred dollars richer than you were."

Joe began to peruse the half-burnt documents but could make little or nothing out of them. He saw his own name and also that of a certain William A. Bodley, and an estate in Iowa was mentioned.

"What do you find, Joe?"

"I can't tell you, Ned. The papers are too badly burnt."

"Let me look at them."

Our hero was willing, and the two boys spent an hour in trying to decipher the documents.

"It is certainly a puzzle," said the rich boy. "Why not let my father look over them?"

Joe was willing, and after wrapping up the documents with care, and pocketing the hundred dollars in gold, Joe led the way back to the boat. The wreck of the blue box was left behind, for it was rusty and worthless.

That evening Mr. Talmadge, Ned and Joe spent two hours in going over the documents and trying to supply the parts which had been rotted or burnt away. They were only successful in part.

"I do not wish to say much about this, Joe," said Ned's father. "But it would seem from these papers that you are the son of one William A. Bodley, who at one time owned a farm in Iowa, in the township of Millville. Did you ever hear Hiram Bodley speak of this?"

"Never."

"We might write to the authorities at Millville and see what they have to say."

"I wish you'd do it. They may pay more attention to you than to a boy."

"I'll write at once."

"Father, hadn't Joe better stay here until we get a reply?" put in Ned.

"He may do so and welcome," answered Mr. Talmadge.

The letter was dispatched the next day and our hero waited anxiously for the reply. It came five days later and was as follows:

"Your letter of inquiry received. There was a William A. Bodley in this township twelve years ago. He sold his farm to a man named Augustus Greggs and then disappeared. Before he sold out he lost his wife and several children by sickness. Nobody here seems to know what became of him. "Joseph Korn."

"That is short and to the point," said Mr. Talmadge, "but it is not satisfying. It does not state if this William A. Bodley had any relatives so far as known."

"I guess the authorities did not want to bother about the matter," said Joe.

"Why don't you visit Millville, Joe?" questioned Ned.

"I was thinking I could do that. It wouldn't cost a fortune, and I've got that hundred dollars in gold to fall back on, besides my regular savings."

"You might learn something to your advantage," came from Mr. Talmadge. "I think it would be money well spent."

"Father, can't I go with Joe?" asked Ned.

"No, Ned, you must attend to your school duties."

"Then, Joe, you must send me full particulars by mail," said the rich boy.

"Of course I'll do that, Ned," replied our hero.

It was arranged that Joe should leave Riverside on Monday and Ned went to the depot to see him off.

"I wish you the best of luck, Joe!" called out Ned, as the train left the station. "I don't know of a fellow who deserves better luck than you do!"

CHAPTER XXV.

JOE VISITS CHICAGO.

Joe found Millville a sleepy town of three or four hundred inhabitants. There was one main street containing two blocks of stores, a blacksmith shop, a creamery and two churches.

When he stepped off the train our hero was eyed sharply by the loungers about the platform.

"Anything I can' do for you?" asked one of the men, the driver of the local stage.

"Will you tell me where Mr. Joseph Korn lives?"

"Joe lives up in the brown house yonder. But he ain't home now. He's doing a job of carpentering."

"Can you tell me where?"

"Up to the Widow Fallow's place. Take you there for ten cents."

"Very well," and our hero jumped into the rickety turnout which went by the name of the Millville stage.

The drive was not a long one and soon they came to a

halt in front of a residence where a man wearing a carpenter's apron was mending a broken-down porch.

"There's Joe," said the stage driver, laconically.

The man looked up in wonder when Joe approached him. He dropped his hammer and stood with his arms on his hips.

"This is Mr. Joseph Korn, I believe?"

"That's me, young man."

"I am Joe Bodley. You wrote to Mr. Talmadge, of Riverside, a few days ago. I came on to find out what I could about a Mr. William A. Bodley who used to live here."

"Oh, yes! Well, young man, I can't tell you much more 'n I did in that letter. Bodley sold out, house, goods and everything, and left for parts unknown."

"Did he have any relatives around here?"

"Not when he left. He had a wife and three children - a girl and two boys - but they died."

"Did you ever hear of any relatives coming to see him - a man named Hiram Bodley?"

"Not me - but Augustus Greggs - who bought his farm - might know about it."

"I'll take you to the Greggs' farm for ten cents," put in the stage driver.

Again a bargain was struck, and a drive of ten minutes brought them to the farm, located on the outskirts of Millville. They found the farm owner at work by his wood pile, sawing wood. He was a pleasant appearing individual.

"Come into the house," he said putting down his saw. "I'm glad to see you," and when our hero had entered the little farmhouse he was introduced to Mrs. Greggs and two grown-up sons, all of whom made him feel thoroughly at home.

"To tell the truth," said Mr. Greggs, "I did not know William Bodley very well. I came here looking for a farm and heard this was for sale, and struck a bargain with him."

"Was he alone at that time?" questioned Joe.

"He was, and his trouble seemed to have made him a bit queer - not but what he knew what he was doing."

"Did you learn anything about his family?"

"He had lost his wife and two children by disease. What had happened to the other child was something of a mystery. I rather supposed it had died while away from home, but I was not sure."

"Have you any idea at all what became of William Bodley?"

"Not exactly. Once I met a man in Pittsburg who had met a man of that name in Idaho, among the mines. Both of us wondered if that William A. Bodley was the same that I had bought my farm from."

"Did he say what part of Idaho?"

"He did, but I have forgotten now. Do you think he was a relative of yours?"

"I don't know what to think. It may be that he was my father.

"Your father?"

"Yes," and Joe told his story and mentioned the documents found in the blue tin box.

"It does look as if he might be your father," said Augustus Greggs. "Maybe you're the child that was away from home at the time his other children and his wife died."

"Do you think anybody else in this village would know anything more about this William Bodley?"

"No, I don't. But it won't do any harm to ask around. That stage driver knows all the old inhabitants. Perhaps some of them can tell you something worth while."

Upon urgent invitation, Joe took dinner at the Greggs' farm and then set out to visit a number of folks who had lived in Millville and vicinity for many years. All remembered William A. Bodley and his family, but not one could tell what had become of the man after he had sold out and gone away.

"Maybe you had better advertise for him," suggested one man.

"It will cost a good deal to advertise all over the United

States," replied Joe; "and for all I know he may be dead or out of the country."

Joe remained in Millville two days and then took the train back to the East. Ned was the first to greet him on his return to Riverside.

"What luck?" he asked, anxiously.

"None whatever," was the sober answer.

"Oh, Joe, that's too bad!"

"I am afraid I am stumped, Ned."

They walked to the Talmadge mansion, and that evening talked the matter over with Ned's father.

"I will arrange to have an advertisement inserted in a leading paper of each of our big cities," said Mr. Talmadge. "That will cost something, but not a fortune."

"You must let me pay for it," said our hero.

"No, Joe, you can put this down to Ned's credit - you two are such good chums," and Mr. Talmadge smiled quietly.

The advertisements were sent out the following day, through an advertising agent, and all waited for over two weeks for some reply, but none came.

"It's no use," said Joe, and it must be admitted that he was much downcast.

In the meantime he had seen Andrew Mallison and the hotel man said he would willingly hire him for the summer as soon as the season opened, and also give Frank Randolph a situation.

"You had better be my guest until that time," said Ned to our hero, when he heard of this.

"Thank you, Ned, but I don't wish to remain idle so long."

The very next mail after this talk brought news for our hero. A letter came from Maurice Vane, asking him if he wished to go to Montana.

"I am now certain that that mine is valuable," wrote the gentleman. "I am going to start West next Monday. If you wish to go with me I will pay your fare and allow you a salary of ten dollars per week to start on. I think later on, I will have a good opening for you."

"That settles it, I am going West!" cried Joe, as he showed the letter to his chum.

"Well, I don't blame you," was the reply. "I know just how nice it is out there. You'll be sure to get along."

Before going to bed Joe wired his acceptance of the offer, and in the morning received a telegram from Maurice Vane, asking him to go to Chicago, to the Palmer House.

"That settles it, I'm off," said our hero, and bought a ticket for the great city by the lakes without delay. Then he said good-bye to the Talmadges and the Gussings, and boarded the train at sundown.

Joe was now getting used to traveling and no longer felt green and out of place. He had engaged a berth, and took his ease until it was time to go to bed. Arriving at Chicago he made his way without delay to the Palmer House.

He found the hotel crowded and had some difficulty in getting a room. Mr. Maurice Vane had not yet arrived.

"I guess I'll leave a note for him," thought our hero, and sauntered into the reading-room to pen the communication.

While Joe was writing, two men came into the room and sat down behind a pillar that was close at hand. They were in earnest conversation and he could not help but catch what was said.

"You say he is coming West?" said one of the pair.

"Yes, - he started yesterday."

"And he has found out that the mine is really valuable?"

"I think so. Anyway he is quite excited about it. He sent a telegram to that boy, too."

"The hotel boy you mean?"

"Yes."

So the talk ran on and Joe at length got up to take a look at the two men. They were Gaff Caven and Pat Malone. At once our hero drew out of sight again.

"How can you get the best of Vane, Gaff?" asked Malone, after a pause.

"There is but one way, Malone."

"And that is?"

"Can I trust you?"

"Haven't you trusted me before?"

"We must - " Caven paused. "We won't talk about it in this public place. Come to my room and I'll lay my plan before you."

Then the two arose and left the reading-room as rapidly as they had entered it.

CHAPTER XXVI.

HOW A SATCHEL DISAPPEARED.

"They certainly mean mischief," Joe told himself, after the two men had vanished. He saw them enter an elevator, but did not know at what floor they alighted.

Looking over the hotel register he was unable to find the names of either Caven or Malone, or even Ball. Evidently the rascals were traveling under other names now.

"They'll bear watching," he concluded. "I must put Mr. Vane on guard as soon as he comes in."

He gave up the idea of leaving a note and took his station in the corridor of the hotel. After waiting about two hours he saw a well-known form approaching, dress-suit case in hand.

"Mr. Vane!"

"Oh, Joe, so you're here already! I'm glad I won't have to wait for you."

"I'm afraid you won't be able to get a room, Mr. Vane. But you can have mine."

"I telegraphed ahead for a room, Joe."

"Do you know that your enemies are here?" went on our hero.

"My enemies?"

"Gaff Caven and Pat Malone. But they are traveling under other names."

"Have they seen you?"

"I think not, sir."

Mr. Vane soon had his room assigned to him and he and our hero passed up in the elevator. As soon as they were in the apartment by themselves, Joe related what he had seen and heard.

"They are certainly on my trail," mused Maurice Vane. "And they must have kept pretty close or they wouldn't know that I had asked you to accompany me."

"They have some plot, Mr. Vane."

"Have you any idea what it is?"

"No, sir, excepting that they are going to try to do you out of your interest in that mine."

Maurice Vane and Joe talked the matter over for an hour, but without satisfaction. Then they went to the dining room for something to eat.

"We start for Montana in the morning," said the gentleman. "I think the quicker I get on the ground the better it will be for me."

Although Maurice Vane and Joe did not know it, both were shadowed by Caven and Malone. The two rascals had disguised themselves by donning false beards and putting on spectacles.

"They leave in the morning," said Caven. "Malone, we must get tickets for the same train, and, if possible, the same sleeping car."

"It's dangerous work," grumbled Pat Malone.

"If you want to back out, say so, and I'll go it alone."

"I don't want to back out. But we must be careful."

"I'll be careful, don't fear," answered the leader of the evil pair.

At the ticket office of the hotel, Maurice Vane procured the necessary tickets and sleeper accommodations to the town of Golden Pass, Idaho. He did not notice that he was watched. A moment later Gaff Caven stepped up to the desk.

"I want a couple of tickets to Golden Pass, too," he said, carelessly.

"Yes, sir."

"Let me see, what sleeper did that other gentleman take?"

"Number 2, sir - berths 7 and 8."

"Then give me 9 and 10 or 5 and 6," went on Caven.

"9 and 10 - here you are, sir," said the clerk, and made out the berth checks. Without delay Caven hurried away, followed by Malone.

"We'll be in the sleeping compartment right next to that used by Vane and the boy," chuckled Gaff Caven. "Pat, it ought to be dead easy."

"Have you the chloroform?"

"Yes, twice as much as we'll need."

"When can we leave the train?"

"At three o'clock, at a town called Snapwood. We can get another train two hours later, - on the northern route."

All unconscious of being watched so closely, Maurice Vane and Joe rode to the depot and boarded the train when it came along. Joe had been looking for Caven and Malone, but without success.

"I cannot see those men anywhere," he said.

"They are probably in hiding," said his employer.

The train was only half full and for the time being Caven and Malone kept themselves either in the smoking compartment or in the dining car. It was dark when they took their seats, and soon the porter came through to make up the berths for the night.

"I   must   confess   I   am   rather   sleepy,"   said

Maurice Vane.

"So am I," returned our hero. "I am sure I can sleep like a top, no matter how much the car shakes."

"Then both of us may as well go to bed at once."

So it was arranged, and they had the porter put up their berths a few minutes later. Maurice Vane took the lower resting place while our hero climbed to the top.

Although very tired it was some time before Joe could get to sleep. He heard Maurice Vane breathing heavily and knew that his employer must be fast in the land of dreams.

When Joe awoke it was with a peculiar, dizzy feeling in his head.

His eyes pained him not a little and for several minutes he could not remember where he was. Then came a faint recollection of having tried to arise during the night but of being held down.

"I must have been dreaming," he thought. "But it was exactly as if somebody was keeping me down and holding something over my mouth and nose."

He stretched himself and then pushed aside the berth curtain and gazed out into the aisle of the car. The porter was already at work, turning some of the berths into seats once more. Joe saw that it was daylight and consulted the nickel watch he carried.

"Eight o'clock!" he exclaimed. "I've overslept myself sure! Mr. Vane must be up long ago."

He slipped into his clothing and then knocked on the lower berth.

He heard a deep sigh.

"Mr. Vane!"

"Eh? Oh, Joe, is that you? What time is it?"

"Eight o'clock."

"What!" Maurice Vane started up. "I've certainly slept fast enough this trip. Are you getting hungry waiting for me?"

"I just woke up myself."

"Oh!" Maurice Vane stretched himself. "My, how dizzy I am."

"I am dizzy too, sir. It must be from the motion of the car."

"Probably, although I rarely feel so, and I ride a great deal. I feel rather sick at my stomach, too," went on the gentleman, as he began to dress.

Joe had just started to go to the lavatory to wash up when he heard his employer utter an exclamation.

"Joe!"

"Yes, sir!"

"Did you see anything of my satchel?"

"You took it into the berth with you."

"I don't see it."

"It must be somewhere around. I saw it when you went to bed."

"Yes, I put it under my pillow."

Both made a hasty search, but the satchel could not be found. The dress-suit case stood under the seat and Joe's was beside it.

"This is strange. Can I have been robbed?"

"Was there much in that satchel, Mr. Vane?"

"Yes, those mining shares and some other articles of value."

"Then we must find the satchel by all means."

"I'll question the porter about this."

The colored man was called and questioned, but he denied having seen the bag. By this time quite a few passengers became interested.

"Has anybody left this car?" asked Maurice Vane.

"The gen'men that occupied Numbers 9 and 10, sah," said the porter.

"When did they get off?"

" 'Bout three o'clock, sah - when de train stopped

at Snapwood."

"I haven't any tickets for Snapwood," said the conductor, who had appeared on the scene.

"Then they must have had tickets for some other point," said Joe.

"That looks black for them."

The porter was asked to describe the two men and did so, to the best of his ability. Then another search was made, and in a corner, under a seat, a bottle was found, half filled with chloroform.

"It's as plain as day to me," said Maurice Vane. "Joe, I was chloroformed."

"Perhaps I was, too. That's what gave us the dizzy feeling."

"And those two men -"

"Must have been Caven and Malone in disguise," finished our hero.

CHAPTER XXVII.

JOE MAKES A DISCOVERY.

"Who are Caven and Malone?" asked the conductor of the train, while a number of passengers gathered around, to hear what Maurice Vane and our hero might have to say.

"They are two rascals who are trying to do me out of my share of a mine," explained Maurice Vane. "I had my mining shares in that satchel."

"If you wish I'll telegraph back to Snapwood for you," went on the train official.

"How many miles is that?"

"A little over two hundred."

"What is the next stop of this train?"

"Leadington."

"When will we get there?"

"In ten minutes."

A telegram was prepared and sent back to Snapwood

as soon as Leadington was reached. The train was held for five minutes and it was learned that nobody had been seen at the station there at three in the morning, as the night operator and station master were away, there being no passengers to get on the train bound West.

Maurice Vane was much disturbed and did not know what to do.

"To go back and look for them at Snapwood may be a mere waste of time," said he. "On the other hand, I don't feel much like going on while the shares are out of my possession."

"If you wish it, Mr. Vane, I'll go back," said Joe. "You can go ahead, and if anything turns up I will telegraph to you."

This pleased the gentleman, and he said Joe could go back on the very next train. The conductor was again consulted, and our hero left the train bound West a quarter of an hour later.

"Here is some money," said Maurice Vane on parting. "You'll need it." And he handed over two hundred dollars.

"Oh, Mr. Vane! will I need as much as this?"

"Perhaps. If you see those rascals you may have a long chase to capture them. Do not hesitate to spend the money if it appears necessary to do so."

Long before noon our hero was on the way East on a train scheduled to stop at Snapwood. He went without his dress-suit case and carried his money in four different pockets.

The train was almost empty and the riding proved decidedly lonely. In a seat he found an Omaha paper, but he was in no humor for reading. When noon came he took his time eating his dinner, so that the afternoon's ride might not appear so lasting.

About half-past two o'clock the train came to an unexpected halt.

Looking out of the window Joe saw that they were in something of a cut, close to the edge of a woods.

The delay continued, and presently one passenger after another alighted, to learn the meaning of the hold-up. Joe did likewise, and walked through the cut toward the locomotive.

The mystery was easily explained. On one side of the cut the bank had toppled over the tracks, carrying with it two trees of good size. A number of train hands were already at work, sawing the trees into pieces, so that they might be shifted clear of the tracks.

Joe watched the men laboring for a few minutes and then walked up the bank, to get a look at the surroundings. Then he heard a whistle and saw a train approaching from the opposite direction. It came to a halt a few hundred feet away.

As the delay continued our hero walked along the bank of the cut and up to the newly-arrived train. The latter was crowded with passengers, some of whom also got out.

"Did that train stop at Snapwood?" he asked of one of the passengers.

"It did," was the answer.

"Did you see anybody get on?"

"No, but somebody might have gotten on. I wasn't looking."

"Thank you."

"Looking for a friend?"

"No," said Joe, and moved on.

Without delay our hero ran to the front end of the newly-arrived train and got aboard. As he walked through he gave every grown passenger a close look.

At the end of the third car he came upon two suspicious-looking individuals, who were gazing at a bit of paper in the hands of one. Joe came closer and saw that the paper was a mining share.

"Caven and Malone, as sure as fate!" he murmured to himself. "What had I best do next?"

While Joe was trying to make up his mind, Caven chanced to glance up and his eyes fell upon our hero. He gave a cry of dismay and thrust the mining share out of sight.

"What's the matter?" asked Malone in a low tone.

"Look there, Pat! That boy!"

"No!"

"But it is!"

"How did he get on this train?"

"I don't know. But it's unpleasant enough for us."

"Do you suppose Vane is around?" asked Malone, nervously.

"He may be."

The two men stared around the car. Only some women and children were present, the men having gone out to learn the cause of the delay.

"Perhaps we had better get out," went on Malone.

"All right"

They arose, and, satchel in hand, started to leave the train.

"Stop!" cried Joe, and caught Caven by the arm.

"Let go of me, boy!" ejaculated the rascal, and tried to pull himself loose.

"I won't let go, Gaff Caven."

"If you don't, it will be the worse for you! I am not to be trifled with!"

"You must give up that satchel."

"Bah!"

"If you don't, I'm going to have you arrested."

"Who is going to arrest me here?" sneered the man who had robbed Maurice Vane. "Don't you know we are miles away from any town?"

"I don't care. Give up the satchel, or I'll call the train hands."

"I'll give up nothing, boy! Stand out of my way!"

Gaff Caven gave Joe a violent shove which sent our hero up against a seat. Then he turned and ran from the car, with Pat Malone ahead of him.

"Stop them!" cried Joe, as soon as he could recover. "Stop the thieves!"

Others took up the cry, but before anything could be done Caven and Malone were out of the car and on to the tracks. Both stared around in perplexity for a second.

"Come on, we can't afford to waste time here!" cried Caven, and ran for the bank of the cut, up which he scrambled hastily, with his confederate at his side.

Joe saw them make the move and was not slow to follow. Near at hand was a tall, western young man, with bronzed features and a general outdoor manner.

"Say!" cried our hero. "Will you help me to catch those two men? They are thieves and I want them arrested. If you'll help me catch them I'll pay you well for your trouble."

"I'll go you, stranger!" answered the western young man, readily. "You are certain of your game?"

"Yes. That satchel has their plunder in it. They robbed a friend of mine."

"This suits me then, friend. We'll round 'em up in short order."

By this time Caven and Malone had gained the woods. Looking back they saw Joe coming behind, accompanied by the westerner.

"He's after us, and he has got somebody to help him," ejaculated Malone.

"Well, I reckon we can run as fast as they can," answered Gaff Caven. "Come ahead!"

He led the way along a trail that ran through the woods and came out on a winding country road. Beyond was another patch of timber.

"This way, Pat," said he. "We'll have to take to the woods again. They are too close for comfort."

"Can't we climb a tree, or hide in a hollow?" questioned the confederate.

"We'll see," said Caven.

They pushed on harder than ever, and passed in among some tall trees. Then they came to a tree that was bent over.

"Up you go," cried Caven, and gave his confederate a boost into the tree. Then he hauled himself up.

"Now climb to the top," he went on, and Malone did as requested. Caven followed suit, and both hid themselves among the thick branches.

"They won't find us here," said Malone, after ten minutes had passed.

"Don't make a noise," whispered Caven.

After that they remained silent. From a great distance came a shouting, and the whistling of locomotives. The trees were being hauled from the car tracks. A little later they heard more whistling and then the two trains passed on their way.

"The trains have gone," whispered Malone. "Do you think the boy got aboard one of them?"

"No, I don't," answered his companion. "He is too determined a lad to give up so easily. He must be still looking for us."

CHAPTER XXVIII.

FROM OUT OF A TREE.

Caven was right, Joe and his newly-made friend were still in the woods, doing their best to locate the two rascals.

They had found the trail but lost it in the patch of tall timber, and were gazing around when they heard the trains leaving the cut.

"There goes our outfit, friend," said the westerner. "And there won't be another train along for several hours."

"It's too bad, but it can't be helped," answered our hero. "But I'll pay you for all time lost, Mr. -"

"Plain Bill Badger is my handle, stranger."

"My name is Joe Bodley."

"What about these two varmin you are after?"

"They were trying to rob a friend of mine of some mining shares," answered Joe, and gave a few details.

"Well, I vow!" cried Bill Badger "That mine is close to

one my dad owns. They say it ain't of much account though."

"Mr. Vane thinks it is valuable. He has had a mining expert go into the matter with great care."

"Then that's a different thing. Were you bound for the mine?"

"Yes, and so was Mr. Vane. We were on the train together when he was robbed."

"I see. I was going out to my dad's mine."

"Then perhaps we can journey together - after we get through here," said Joe.

"I'm willing. I like your looks. Shake." And the pair shook hands.

Although a westerner, Bill Badger knew no more about following a trail than did our hero, consequently they proceeded on their hunt with difficulty.

"Reckon we've missed 'em," said Bill Badger, a while later. "Don't see hide nor hair of 'em anywhere."

"It's too bad if they got away," answered Joe. "Perhaps - What was that?"

The cracking of a tree limb had reached their ears, followed by a cry of alarm. A limb upon which Pat Malone was standing had broken, causing the fellow to slip to another branch below.

"Hush! don't make so much noise!" said Caven,

in alarm.

"Gosh! I thought I was going to tumble, out of the tree to the ground," gasped Malone, when he could catch his breath.

"They are coming - I can see them," whispered Gaff Caven. "Be as quiet as a mouse."

In a moment more Joe and Bill Badger stood directly under the tree.

"I think the noise came from near here," said Joe.

"I agree," answered the westerner.

At that moment our hero looked up and saw a man's arm circling a tree limb far over his head.

"They are up there!" he shouted.

"Sure?"

"Yes, I just saw one of them."

"Then we've got 'em treed," came with a broad grin from Bill Badger. "What's the next turn of the game?"

"We have got to make them both prisoners."

"All right. Have you got a shooting iron?"

"No, but I can get a club."

"Then do it, and I'll use this, if it's necessary," and the young westerner pulled a pistol from his hip pocket.

"I wish we had some ropes, with which to tie them," continued Joe.

"Here's a good big handkerchief."

"That's an idea. My handkerchief is also good and strong."

"You do the pow-wowing and I'll do the shooting, if it's necessary," said Bill Badger.

Joe looked up into the tree again but could see nobody.

"Caven!" he called out. "I know you are up there and I want you to come down."

To this remark and request there was no reply.

"If you don't come down we may begin to fire at you," went on our hero.

"Oh, say, do you think he'll shoot?" whispered Malone, in sudden alarm.

"No; shut up!" returned Caven.

"Are you coming down or not?" went on Joe.

Still there was no reply.

"I'll give 'em a shot to warn 'em" said Bill Badger, and fired into the air at random.

"Don't shoot me!" roared Pat Malone. "Please don't! I'll come down!"

"Well, you come down first. Caven, you stay up there for the present."

After this there was a pause, and presently Pat Malone came down out of the tree looking sheepish enough.

"Up with your hands!" cried Bill Badger, and confronted by the firearms the hands of the rascal went up in a hurry.

Then Joe took his handkerchief and stepped up behind Malone. The hands were lowered and crossed and our hero tied them firmly together at the wrists.

"Now back up to that tree yonder," said our hero. "And don't you dare to move."

"I'll do just as you say," whined Malone. "Only don't shoot me." He was a coward at heart.

"Now, Caven, you come down!" shouted Joe.

"I don't think I care to," answered that rascal, coolly.

"If you don't come down I'll come up after you with my pistol," broke in Bill Badger.

"Maybe I can do a little shooting myself," went on Gaff Caven.

"I'll risk that."

More words followed, but in the end Caven thought it best to descend and did so. Yet his face still wore a look of defiance. He was compelled to turn around, and his hands were also tied behind him.

"Now I want those mining shares, Caven," said Joe.

"I haven't got them."

"Where is the satchel?"

"I threw it away when you started after me."

"Down at the railroad tracks?"

"Yes."

"Don't you believe that," broke in Bill Badger. "At least, not unless he emptied the satchel first."

"Show me the way you came," said Joe.

"Make him point out the satchel, or make him suffer," went on Bill Badger.

"I've got an idea!" cried our hero, suddenly. "Perhaps he left the satchel in the tree."

"That's so. Well, if you want to climb up and look around, I'll watch the pair of 'em."

"Don't let them get away."

"If they try it, they'll go to the hospital or the grave-yard," replied the western young man, significantly.

"The satchel ain't in the tree," growled Caven, but his tone lacked positiveness.

"I'll soon know for certain," said our hero.

He climbed the tree with ease, having been used to such doings when living with the old hermit. As he went from branch to branch he kept his eyes open, and presently saw a bit of leather sticking out of a crotch. He worked his way over and soon had the satchel in his possession.

"How are you making out?" called up Bill Badger.

"I've got it!" shouted our hero, joyfully.

"Got the papers?"

"Yes, - everything," said Joe, after a hasty examination.

"Hang the luck!" muttered Gaff Caven, much chagrined.

Our hero was soon on the ground once more. Here he examined the contents of the satchel with care. Everything was there, and, locking the bag, he slung the strap over his shoulder.

"Now, what's the next move?" queried Bill Badger.

"We ought to have these men locked up. How far is it to the nearest town?"

"Ten or twelve miles, I reckon. I don't know much about the roads."

"Why can't you let us go?" asked Malone. "You've got what you want."

"If I let you go you'll be trying to make more trouble

for Mr. Vane and myself."

"Don't talk to them," growled Caven. "If you want to lock us up, do so!"

He was in an ugly humor and ready for a fight.

"We'll march 'em along," said Bill Badger, and so it was agreed.

CHAPTER XXIX.

THE FATE OF TWO EVILDOERS.

"Are you going to let them arrest us?" whispered Pat Malone, as the whole party moved through the woods towards a wagon road which ran nearly parallel to the railroad tracks.

"Not if I can help it," Caven whispered back. "We must watch our chances."

Half a mile was covered and they came out on the road. It was growing dark and there were signs of a storm in the air.

"It's going to rain," said Joe, and he was right.

"See here, I don't want to get wet to the skin," growled Caven. "I'll catch my death of cold."

"There is a barn just ahead," said Bill Badger. "Let us get inside."

Joe was willing, and soon all were in the barn. It was now raining at a heavy rate and they were glad to be under shelter.

"With a barn there ought to be a house," remarked our

hero. "But I don't see any."

It grew still darker, and the rain came down in perfect sheets. The roof of the barn leaked, and they had to move from one spot to another, to keep out of the drippings.

While this was going on Gaff Caven was working at the handkerchief that bound his wrists and soon had it loose. Pat Malone also liberated himself. Caven winked suggestively at his confederate.

"Watch me," he whispered. "When I give the signal we'll knock 'em both down and run for it."

"But the pistol - " began Malone.

"I'll take care of that."

In moving around the old barn Caven spotted a club and moved close to it. Suddenly he snatched the weapon up and hit Bill Badger on the arm with it. The pistol flew into a corner and went off, sending a bullet into a board.

"Run!" yelled Caven, and leaped for the open doorway. Malone came beside him, and both ran off through the rain as fast as their legs could carry them.

Joe was startled and made after the pair. But at a groan from Bill Badger he paused.

"Are you badly hurt?" he asked.

"He gave me a stiff crack on the arm," growled the young westerner.

Joe ran for the corner and caught up the pistol. Then he leaped for the open doorway.

"Stop, both of you!" he called out. "Stop, or I'll fire!"

"Don't you dare!" shrieked Pat Malone, and ran faster than ever, behind the nearest of the trees. Joe aimed the weapon, but before he could pull the trigger both of the bad men were out of sight.

"Go after them, if you want to," said Bill Badger. "I'll go too."

"You are not badly hurt?" queried our hero, sympathetically.

"No, but if I catch that fellow I'll give it to him good," grumbled the young westerner.

Both now left the barn and made after Caven and Malone. Once they caught sight of the rascals, moving in the direction of the railroad tracks.

"They are going to catch a train if they can!" cried our hero. "I hear one coming."

"It's a freight most likely," was Bill Badger's answer.

He was right, and soon the long line of freight cars hove into sight around a bend and on an upgrade. Far in the distance they beheld Caven and Malone scooting for the train with all speed.

"They are going to make it," sighed Joe. "Too bad!"

They continued to run, but before they could get

anywhere near the tracks they saw Caven leap for the train and get between two of the cars. Then Malone got aboard also, and the freight train passed out of sight through the cut.

"That ends the chase," said Joe, halting. "They were slick to get away."

"If we only knew where they would get off we could send word ahead," suggested his companion.

"Well, we don't know, and after this they will probably keep their eyes wide open and keep out of sight as much as possible. Anyway, I don't think they'll bother Mr. Vane any more."

"It's not likely. I'm a witness to what they were up to," answered the young westerner.

Both Joe and Bill Badger were soaked from the rain and resolved to strike out for the nearest farmhouse or village. They kept along the railroad tracks, and presently came to a shanty where there was a track-walker.

"How far to the nearest village?" asked our hero.

"Half a mile."

"Thank you."

"How is it you are out here in the rain?" went on the track-walker.

"We got off our train and it went off without us."

"Oh, I see. Too bad."

Again our hero and his companion hurried on, and soon came in sight of a small village. They inquired their way to a tavern, and there dried their clothing and procured a good, hot meal, which made both feel much better.

"I am going to send a telegram to Mr. Vane," said Joe, and did so without further delay. He was careful of the satchel and did not leave it out of his sight.

They found they could get a train for the West that evening at seven o'clock and at the proper time hurried to the depot.

"I'm glad I met you," said Joe, to his newly-made friend. "Now, what do you think I owe you for what you did?"

"As we didn't land the fellows in jail you don't owe me anything," said Bill Badger, promptly.

"Oh, yes, I do."

"Well then, you can pay the extra expense, and let that fill the bill."

"I'll certainly do that," said Joe, promptly.

As they rode along Bill Badger told something of himself and of the mine his father owned, and then Joe told something of his own story.

"Did you say your name is Joe Bodley?" asked the young westerner, with deep interest.

"Yes."

"And you are looking for a man by the name of William A. Bodley?"

"I am."

"It seems to me I know a man by that name, although the miners all call him Bill Bodley."

"Where is this Bill Bodley?"

"Out in Montana somewhere. He worked for my father once, about three years ago. He was rather a strange man, about fifty years old. He had white hair and a white beard, and acted as if he had great trouble on his mind."

"You do not know where he is now?"

"No, but perhaps my father knows."

"Then I'm going to see your father as soon as I can," said Joe, decidedly.

"Mind you, I don't say that this Bill Bodley is the man you are after, Joe. I don't want to raise any false hopes."

"Did you ever hear where the man came from?"

"I think he told somebody that he once owned a farm in Kansas or Iowa."

"This William A. Bodley once owned a farm at Millville, Iowa."

"Is that so! Then he may be the same man after all. To tell the truth, he looked a little bit like you."

"Was he a good man?" asked Joe, eagerly.

"Yes, indeed. But some of the men poked fun at him because he was so silent and strange at times. I liked him and so did father. He left us to go prospecting in the mountains."

Thus the talk ran on for half an hour, when the train came to a sudden halt.

"Are we at a station?" asked Bill Badger.

"I don't know," said Joe.

Both looked out of the window but could see nothing except hills and forests.

"We are in the foothills," said the young westerner. "Something must be wrong on the tracks."

"More fallen trees perhaps."

"Or a landslide. They have them sometimes, when it rains as hard as it did to-day."

They left the car with some others and soon learned that there had been a freight collision ahead and that half a dozen freight cars had been smashed to splinters.

"Do you think it can be the freight that Caven and Malone boarded?" came from our hero, on hearing this news.

"It might be," answered Bill Badger. "Let us take a look. Our train won't move for hours now."

They walked to the scene of the wreck. One of the cars had been burnt up but the conflagration was now under control and a wrecking crew was already at work clearing the tracks so that they might be used.

"Anybody hurt?" asked Joe of a train hand.

"Yes, two men killed. They were riding between the cars."

"Tramps?"

"They didn't look like tramps. But they hadn't any right to ride on the freight."

"Where are they?"

"Over in the shanty yonder."

With a queer sensation in his heart Joe walked to the little building, accompanied by Bill Badger. A curious crowd was around and they had to force their way to the front.

One look was enough. Gaff Caven and Pat Malone lay there, cold in death. They had paid the penalty of their crimes on earth and gone to the final judgment.

CHAPTER XXX.

CONCLUSION.

"Let us go away!" whispered Joe, and moved out of the gathering without delay.

"It was sure rough on 'em," was Bill Badger's comment.

"Oh, it was awful!" cried our hero. "I - I didn't expect this, did you?"

"Nobody did. It must have come sudden like on to 'em."

"It makes me sick at heart to think of it. I - I hope it wasn't our fault."

"Not at all. If they hadn't broke away they'd be alive this minute. They'll never bother you or your friend again, Joe."

Our hero felt weak at the knees and was glad enough to go back to the train, where he sank into his seat. He scarcely said another word until the wreck was cleared away and they were once more on their journey.

"I reckon you are glad you got the satchel before this

happened," remarked Bill Badger, when they were preparing to retire.

"Yes. But I - I wish they had gotten away. It's awful to think they are dead - and with such bad doings to their credit."

Joe did not sleep very well and he was up early in the morning and out on the rear platform, drinking in the fresh air. He felt as if he had passed through some fearful nightmare.

"How do you like this climate?" asked Bill Badger, as he came out. "Ain't it just glorious?"

"It certainly is," said Joe, and he remembered what Ned had told him. "I don't wonder some folks like it better than the East."

"Oh, the East can't compare to it," answered Bill Badger. "Why I was once down to New York and Boston, and the crowd and confusion and smoke and smells made me sick for a week! Give me the pure mountain air every time!"

The day proved a pleasant one and when he did not remember the tragedy that had occurred our hero enjoyed the ride and the wild scenery.

At last Golden Pass was reached, late at night, and they got off in a crowd of people.

"Joe!"

"Mr. Vane!" was the answering cry, and soon the two were shaking hands. "Let me introduce a new friend,

Mr. Bill Badger."

"Glad to know you."

"Mr. Badger helped me get back your satchel," went on our hero.

"Then I am deeply indebted to him."

"In that case, just drop the mister from my name," drawled the young westerner. "Joe tells me you have a mine up here. My father has one, too - the Mary Jennie, next to the Royal Flush."

"Oh, yes, I know the mine, and I have met your father," said Maurice Vane.

They walked to a hotel, and there Joe and his young western friend told their stories, to which Maurice Vane listened with keen interest. The gentleman was shocked to learn of the sudden death of Caven and Malone.

"It was certainly a sad ending for them," said he. "But, as Badger says, they had nobody but themselves to blame for it."

Maurice Vane was extremely glad to get back his mining shares and thanked Bill Badger warmly for what he had done.

"Don't you mention it," said the young westerner. "I'm going to hunt up dad now. When you get time, call and see us."

"I'm coming up soon, to find out about that Bill

Bodley," said Joe.

As late as it was Joe listened to what Maurice Vane had to tell.

"Now that Caven and Malone are gone I do not anticipate further trouble at the mine," said the gentleman. "I am in practical possession of all the shares, and shall have a clear title to the whole property inside of a few weeks."

When Joe told him what Bill Badger had had to say about a certain man called Bill Bodley he was much interested.

"Yes, you must find out about this man at once," said he. "I will help you, as soon as certain matters are settled."

The next morning proved a busy one and Joe got no time to call upon Bill Badger's father. He visited the mine and looked over it with interest.

During the middle of the afternoon he went back to town on an errand for Mr. Vane. He was passing a cabin on the outskirts when he heard loud words and a struggle.

"Let me go, you ruffian!" cried a weak voice. "Leave that money alone!"

"You shut up, old man!" was the answer. "The money is all right."

"You are trying to rob me!"

Then there was another struggle, and suddenly a door burst open and a man leaped into the roadway. At sight of him Joe came to a halt. The fellow was Bill Butts, the man who had tried to swindle Josiah Bean.

"Stop him!" came from the cabin. "He has my gold!"

"Stop!" cried Joe, and ran up to Butts. The next moment man and boy tripped and fell, but, luckily, our hero was on top.

"Let me go!" growled the man.

"So we meet again, Butts!" cried Joe.

The man stared in amazement and then began to struggle. Seeing this, Joe doubled up his fists and gave him a blow in the nose and in the right eye, which caused him to roar with pain.

"That's right!" came from the doorway of the cabin. "Give it to him! Make him give me my gold!"

"Give up the gold," ordered Joe.

"There it is!" growled Bill Butts, and threw a buckskin bag towards the cabin. The man from within caught it up and stowed it away in his pocket.

"Shall I call a policeman?" asked Joe.

"I don't know," said the man from the cabin. He wore a troubled face and had white hair and a white beard. "It may be - Wha - where did you come from?" he gasped.

"Where did I come from?" asked Joe.

"Yes! yes! Answer me quickly! You are - you must be a ghost! I saw you in my dreams last week!"

"I don't understand you," said Joe, and arose slowly to his feet, at which Bill Butts did likewise and began to retreat. "I never met you before."

"No? It's queer." The man brushed his hand over his forehead. "Yes, I must be dreaming. But I am glad I got my gold back."

"So am I, but the rascal has run away."

"Never mind, let him go."

"What makes you think you've seen me before?" questioned Joe, and his breath came thick and fast.

"I - er - I don't know. You mustn't mind me - I have queer spells at times. You see, I had a whole lot of trouble once, and when I get to thinking about it - " The man did not finish.

"May I ask your name?" asked Joe, and his voice trembled in spite of his efforts at self-control.

"Sure you can. It's Bill Bodley."

"William A. Bodley?"

"Yes. But how do you happen to know my full name?"

"Did you once own a farm in Millville, Iowa?"

"I had a farm in Iowa, yes. It was Millville Center in those days."

Joe drew closer and looked at the man with care and emotion.

"Did you ever have a brother named Hiram Bodley?"

"I did - but he has been dead for years."

"No, Hiram Bodley died only a short time ago," answered Joe. "I used to live with him. My name is Joe Bodley. He told me I was his nephew."

"You his nephew! Hiram Bodley's nephew! We didn't have any brothers or sisters, and he was a bachelor!"

"I know he was a bachelor. But I don't know - " Joe paused.

"He told me Joe died, at least I got a letter from somebody to that effect. But I was near crazy just then, and I can't remember exactly how it was. I lost my wife and two children and then I guess I about lost my mind for a spell. I sold out, and the next thing I knew I was roving around the mountains and in rags. Then I took to mining, and now I've got a mine of my own, up yonder in the mountains. Come in and talk this over."

Joe entered the cabin and sat down, and William Bodley plied him with questions, all of which he answered to the best of his ability.

"There was a blue tin box I had," said he, presently, "that contained some documents that were mine."

"A blue tin box!" ejaculated Joe. "Hiram Bodley had it and it got lost. I found it a long time afterwards and some parts of the documents were destroyed. I have the rest in my suit case at the hotel."

"Can I see those papers?"

"Certainly."

"Perhaps you are my son, Joe?"

"Perhaps I am, sir."

They went to the hotel, and the documents were produced. Then William Bodley brought out some letters he possessed. Man and boy went over everything with care.

"You must be my son!" cried William Bodley. "Thank heaven you are found!" And they shook hands warmly.

He told Joe to move over to the cabin, and our hero did so. It was a neat and clean place and soon Joe felt at home. Then he heard his father's tale in detail - an odd and wonderful story - of great trials and hardship.

"There will always be something of a mystery about this," said William Bodley. "But, no matter, so long as I have you with me."

"Uncle Hiram was a queer stick," answered Joe. "I suppose if he was alive he could explain many things." And in this Joe was correct.

Let us add a few words more and then draw our tale to a close.

When Joe told Maurice Vane how he had found a father the gentlemen was much astonished. So were the

Badgers, but all were glad matters had ended so well.

It was found that William Bodley's mine was a valuable one. The ore in it was about equal to the ore in the mine owned by Maurice Vane, and this was likewise equal to that in the mine run by Mr. Badger.

After some conversation on the subject it was agreed by all the interested parties to form a new company, embracing all the mines. Of the shares of this new concern, one-third went to Maurice Vane, one-third to the Badgers, and one-third to William Bodley and Joe. The necessary machinery was duly installed, and to-day the new company is making money fast.

On the day after his trouble with Mr. Bodley, Bill Butts disappeared from town. But a week later he was arrested in Denver and sent to jail for two years for swindling a ranchman.

During the following summer Joe received a visit from his old friend Ned, and the two boys had a delightful time together. In the meantime Joe spent half of his time at the mine and half over his books, for he was determined to get a good education.

For a long time William Bodley had been in feeble health, but with the coming of Joe on the scene he began to mend rapidly, and was soon as hale and hearty as anybody. He was an expert miner, and was made general superintendent for the new company.

To-day Joe has a good education and is rich, but come what may, it is not likely that he will forget those days when he was known as "Joe the Hotel Boy."